A Boy from Makkah

By
Dr. Muhammad Abdo Yamani

IQRA'
International Educational Foundation
Chicago

Part of a Comprehensive and Systematic Program of Islamic Studies

Program of Literature

Junior / Senior

A Boy from Makkah

Chief Program Editors

Dr. Abidullah al-Ansari Ghazi
Ph.D., Comparative Religions
Harvard University

Tasneema Khatoon Ghazi
Ph.D., Curriculum-Reading
University of Minnesota

Language Editing

K.S. Hammer
M.A., Indiana University

Khadija H. Mohiuddin
B.A., DePaul University

Sven T. De Backer
B.A., Antwerp University

Designer

Aliuddin Khaja

Illustrator

'Abdallah Lipton

Library of Congress Catalog Card Number 99-080151
ISBN 1-56316-057-9

IQRA' NOTE

IQRA' International Educational Foundation is honored to make available the novel *A Boy from Makkah* (an English translation of the Arabic novel *al-Yad as-Suflah* [The Lower Hand]) by Dr. Abdo Yamani. Dr. Yamani is one of the top academics and nation builders of Saudi Arabia whose intellectual insights and practical efforts have helped forge modern Saudi society. He is an educator, writer, Islamic scholar, businessman, philanthropist, and above all, a fine example of Islamic piety and Arab generosity. His broad outlook on life has enriched Saudi life and interpreted it for both the Arab and non-Arab worlds. His credentials are noteworthy having served as president of King 'Abd al-'Aziz University as well as information minister of the Kingdom of Saudi Arabia. Currently, among his many designations, he chairs two major educational organizations: IQRA' Charitable Society, Jeddah and IQRA' International Educational Foundation, Chicago.

Dr. Yamani is an eloquent writer and storyteller. His stories describe the evolution of modern Saudi society and the social, economic, and political changes that oil wealth has brought to this traditional society. He is not only an interpreter of the social development but also a designer of that change and one who participates in setting the course for future developments. His style of writing is simple; his plot is factual; and his characters represent the living ethos of modern Saudi Arabia. He weaves the Arabian environment and Islamic traditions with an emerging world horizon. Indeed, Dr. Yamani's delightful novel comes to the English speaking world at an appropriate moment in history when globalization and cross-cultural exchanges are on the rise. For inquisitive minds, their cultural curiosities may be satisfied through a novel such as this that captures the essence of a rich Arab-Muslim culture in transition.

This story unfolds the biography of a young boy who was deprived of opportunities but whose persistent efforts and fortunate encounters with the generosity of Makkan patrons achieve him high distinctions and a bright career. Still, this novel goes beyond the realm of physical struggle and shows how one boy's faith, his patience and perseverance win him success in his career and a lasting love. At long last has arrived a novel that embodies the Arab-Islamic qualities of modesty and sincerity that love really entails. This story, in short, is a social history of modern Arab society, through which we can see its social evolution and personal advancement.

We hope that all our readers will find this an interesting and insightful reading to understand the developments in both the social and intellectual life of a country significant both to Muslims (for its religious sanctity) and non-Muslims (for its enormous economic potential and political influence). We are confident that *A Boy from Makkah* will soon become a treasured favorite in every library.

Chief Editors
IQRA' International Educational Foundation
January 1, 2002

CONTENTS

Chapter One

Chapter One

"We're almost there, Ahmad!" my father said, "We're almost in Makkah!" The cheerful tone was apparently meant to encourage me to walk on, though my father himself looked exhausted, having covered such a long road from our native village, Beni Faham, on foot. Jogging along by his side, I remembered that we had

transport only for a very short distance. It was all my father, God rest his soul, could afford: he was destitute. I was, perhaps, equally tired, but, being only nine and absorbed as I was in reveries that bordered on the fantastic, I could take physical hardship in my stride. One reverie led to another, from actually being inside the Grand Mosque--that vast and awesome place which houses the Ka'bah, the holiest Muslim shrine--to walking through the streets of Makkah, lined with modern buildings, and enjoying its rich markets! I had heard a lot about Makkah and had seen in my mind's eye a Makkah full of delicious food, sweets, peanuts, and rich desserts. Villagers returning from Makkah always brought samples of these, and I had always devoured my portion with great relish, particularly that "special" dessert aptly called "pudding of Paradise." A child's imagination couldn't run too wild, could it?

We walked on, perhaps picking up speed after my father's encouraging remark, while all the time cars seemed to whiz past us: lorries, pick-ups and buses. I had known these only by name. But we did take a cab--a pick-up, actually--for part of our journey to Makkah. It was quite an experience: my father and I were squeezed into the crowded vehicle and, when it had covered the distance "bought" by the little money father had paid, we were asked to get off and continue on foot. It was all behind us now . . . we were actually on the outskirts of Makkah!

We climbed a hill--one of the many surrounding the holy city--and, when we reached the top, my father stopped. With one hand on my shoulder, his eyes strained towards a far away place, he pointed to it and whispered in pious tones, "This is the house of God."

It was like a revelation. I seemed to forget everything around me, even my very self, and melt into the spectacle. I forgot the family I had left behind, my brothers and friends in Beni Faham, my life in that village and our little house in the open fields. I could see nothing except Makkah, now in full view, the Grand Mosque with its high minarets and tall buildings, and the House of God, in its midst, in all its awesome splendor. The image passed into my soul forever. I felt I was getting lighter and lighter, that I soared into space and, bird-like, beat my trilled wings over that shrine. A mysterious sense made me almost ecstatic and, unconsciously, tears began to trickle down my face. The place suddenly felt so near, so familiar, though I had never been to it before.

A light tap on my shoulder brought me back to reality. My father beckoned me to carry on, walking down the hill and stepping into the holy city. I had forgotten all about the sought-after sweets.

My father stopped at a place where people were performing the rites of ablution. There were taps, which they turned on and water came down. I was simply bewildered. Back home at the village we had other means of getting water for ablution and drinking, but the taps . . . well! My father realized I needed help and immediately offered it; soon I was able to get the water I needed and, transported by the joy of being at the threshold of the Grand Mosque itself, I quickly pushed my way through into the vast open area in the middle. My eyes were fixed on the Ka'bah and I had no other thought but to rush to it and kiss the holy shrine. The House of God was only a few yards away!

"Come on then," my father said, "Let us go 'round the Ka'bah." His voice recalled me from my reverie--and surprised me. I had always thought that on entering a mosque one said a little prayer as a reverential rite--but to go around the shrine? Conscious of my surprise, my father smiled reassuringly and said, "That is right, Ahmad! You say a little prayer on entering any other mosque, but in reverence to the Grand Mosque you go around the Ka'bah." We went around at a vigorous pace and every time I passed the Yemeni corner and the black stone I stopped to kiss them. My father was happy to let go of my hand as I rushed to do so, then waited for me to rejoin him.

The rounds done, we stopped at the Stone of Ismail and said a prayer, then at the Shrine of Ibrahim and said another, each taking longer than usual. The words seemed to come from the deepest recess of my soul, and I felt almost exhausted. The intensity of the spiritual experience was too much for me: having lived for so long with the idea of the holy shrine, I was now actually looking at it. The sight possessed me entirely.

My father again took me by the hand and, together, we stopped at al-Multazam. He touched the door with both hands then walked a few steps to a spot midway. I stood on tiptoe but could not reach the door; my father lifted me. I touched it and we said a prayer for my mother, my brothers, and the imam of our mosque in Beni Faham. My prayers felt genuine and warm--I was doing something for those who loved and helped me.

Leaving the Grand Mosque, I felt my heart radiate with light. It was like being reborn. I walked lightly on the ground, as though the long journey on foot had never happened. But I had had no food since we left Beni Faham early that morning and I was famished.

Suddenly we were in the marketplace. The delicious smell of food being offered at many shops, right and left was irresistible! I tugged at my father's hand and said playfully, "Should we fast, father, now we've gone round the Ka'bah, or are we allowed to have a bite?" My father was familiar with my way of making a request; he did not answer but simply swerved into a side street and, laughing down on me, stopped at a small café. People were eating, drinking tea, and smoking nargiles. It was very small and catered to those who could not afford a restaurant. In no time at all food was served, eaten, and paid for. I had a lovely sense of well being! Tea, however, was yet to be served--the special treat I have always waited for. I had my own ways of making it and would miss a good meal for my cup of tea, so to speak. I either added mint, lemon juice, lemon tree leaves, or, indeed, rose leaves! I would settle for no less and never took any notice of my family's significant smiles, or sneers, as I prepared it.

Tea was served and I started to sip it with great relish. I thought that the novel pleasures of Makkah would easily make up for the lost pleasure of being with family at home. The light that filled my heart in the Grand Mosque was still a source of reassurance, which would never be surpassed. I was very happy.

Where were we going to spend the night? It was not, apparently, a problem. My father took me to Al-Beeban district where we hired two deck chairs at one of the many cafes to be found everywhere in Makkah, and with them two good quilts. Without further ado, we were tucked in comfortably and fell asleep in a matter of seconds.

I was woken up by the Muezzin's voice, calling for the dawn prayers. Before I opened my eyes, I felt a touch on my shoulder. "Ahmad, wake up," my father said. "We have to hurry! We don't want to miss the dawn prayers at the Grand Mosque, do we?"

Half asleep, almost dazed, I looked up but could not reply. I thought of the distance we had to cover the day before to arrive at this place, and was horrified by the prospect of having to do it again so early in the morning. "I am awake, father," I muttered, "It's just the distance! Don't you think it's a very long road?" "All right then," my father said with a sigh, "we'll take the bus."

Taking the bus was a new experience. I had often seen it passing by our village, but I had never actually stepped into it, as I had never left my village before. On the bus, I felt the soft, smooth comfortable seat. How different, I thought, from that pick-up which we took for part of the journey yesterday! Then I saw the House of God once again. It was different this time, for now the minarets were silhouetted against the colors of the new day in the eastern sky. The delicate contours were imprinted on my mind forever. For all the novelty and the freshness of foreign countries that I later came to visit, I never again had that same feeling of being at the threshold of a new day, a new spiritual adventure, at once exciting and reassuring, as I felt that morning in Makkah.

The prayers performed, I asked my father if I could go around the Ka'bah a few more times. I was left to my own thoughts as I made the rounds. I wondered about the secret of that strange happiness which bordered on ecstasy. I could not even quite describe the feeling, much less explain it. As we left the Grand Mosque, I was content to feel this way as I left, never to find out why.

We had breakfast at the same café as the night before--a dish of beans and bread. We sat together silently for some time. My father's face was serious and almost stern. I wanted to ask him whether there was anything else we would do in town but did not dare. I simply watched him carefully and came more and more to suspect that he wanted to approach an unusual subject. After a while, he broke the silence. "Listen, Ahmad. This is a new day. It's your first day in Makkah, where you will work and help me support our family with your wages. You know, my son, I am sure, how difficult life has become for us back home . . ."

There was nothing I could say. I simply nodded

as I considered my father's words. I thought of my village, my family, and friends. I knew that my early childhood had been spent in perfect security; none of us were ever concerned with how my father earned enough money to support us. I, for one, had never thought about it. Now, it all came to life.

The little revenue from farming our patch of land had never been enough, and my father had always had to undertake a variety of other works for the little extra that we could get. Sometimes he helped the other farmers; sometimes he took their crops to sell in Jeddah or Makkah, in return for a small commission. No amount of extra money seemed enough, however, as our family grew bigger and life more expensive. This was why my father had brought me over to Makkah to work. He must have many friends and acquaintances here, I thought, to help him in this. I was silent perhaps for too long, and my father looked worried. Maybe he wondered whether I was hesitant or reluctant, and his tone was unprecedently serious, "You're the eldest, Ahmad. You're the most mature, the most intelligent. I didn't think that I would have to explain to you what our situation is, the real position of . . ."

I suddenly looked at him and smiled; we needed no further words. I was, in fact, touched by his apologetic tone as I saw no reason at all for apology. He smiled back, then kissed me and whispered, "God bless you my son."

"Did you think I would disobey you? Did you think I could even go against your will?"

"I know you wouldn't . . ."

"But Father, please, there's one thing I want . . . one little thing . . ."

"What is it?"

"To work with you, Father, at the same place! I have never been away from you; it's hard enough having to leave Mother . . ."

The silence this time was deep. My words apparently made a deep impression on him; he looked pained and appeared to be fighting back the tears in his eyes. His voice almost choked though he did his best to make it sound normal. "I wish it were possible, Ahmad. Alas! What must be, must be! But don't worry, my son, you'll be working at a safe place, with a family who will be like your own. You must be devoted in their service to win their confidence."

"Oh, no!" I answered quickly, "never like my own! One's family is one's family, and strangers are strangers! I don't think that anyone could look after me like you or my mother!"

I suddenly realized that I was not making it any easier for him. He was in great pain as it was and now looked terribly sad. "I am sure, Ahmad," he said, taking my hand in his, "you'll be quite happy in your new life. I shall see you often, God willing, since I often come to Makkah as you know. Let's go then, shall we? Be a man!" We left the café, and for a while seemed to be walking aimlessly through the narrow winding streets of Makkah. Then, unexpectedly, we stopped at a small shop where an old man sat.

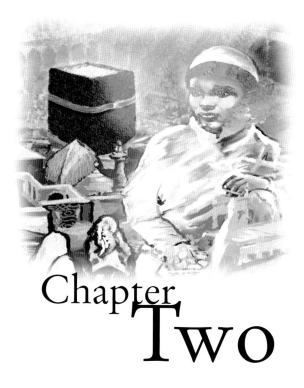

Chapter
Two

Chapter Two

"Peace be with you Sheikh Ba Qays!" my father greeted this old man. The man seemed unwell, though his voice was loud and vigorous as he returned my father's greeting. "Peace be with you Ayda, welcome!" he said. He looked at me searchingly then asked my father if I was his son. My father nodded and I felt a little

awkward. Rather shyly, I greeted Sheikh Ba Qays.
"Welcome . . . welcome!" he returned. Quickly, my
father said, "I have brought him over to Makkah in
the hope that you, Sheikh Ba Qays, will find him a
job."

The man looked interested as he answered,
"You've come at the right time! Sheikh Salah is looking for a boy to work at his home. He's actually
looking for a young boy of your son's age." Pausing
for a moment, Sheikh Ba Qays continued in the significant tone of a man breaking an important piece of
news.

"He's offering good wages. And they are good
people, as you know."

"That's fine Sheikh Ba Qays. I have no objection," my father nodded.

The conversation had come to an end. It was
as though everything had been signed and sealed.
Looking at one, then the other, I felt that I understood nothing. I had many questions to ask. To
begin with, I didn't know what kind of life I would be
leading. I also wondered how I would see my father
afterwards. Lots of questions jostled in my mind and
I was unable, or rather not in a position, to talk. I
hoped that my questions would be answered in due
course. I sat on a big stone in front of the shop and
decided to wait and see. Ba Qays apparently had
been in the middle of some sums, which he had to
attend to first. When he finished he called one of the
assistants at the back of the shop, and in the tone of a
merchant who wants some goods delivered to a customer

he said, "Take this boy--his name is Ahmad Bin Ayda--to the house of Sheikh Salah. Tell him it's the boy he's been asking for." Ba Qays went back to his arithmetic as though the matter had ended there. He believed that he had fulfilled his part of the bargain by finding the boy Sheikh Salah had wanted.

I was bewildered. I didn't know what to do. I looked at my father but felt he was avoiding my eyes. Suddenly I felt the hand of the assistant pulling at mine, as he said in equally indifferent tones, "Let's go then, boy!" I couldn't move. I saw a huge abyss--a sudden precipice opening before me. What was my future life to be?

I could, the nine-year-old boy that was, see it all: separation from father, family and village, and a new life upon which I was suddenly being launched. Unconsciously I clung fast to my father's hand. He freed his hand, then put both hands on my shoulders and looked at me steadily as though he wanted to see as much of me as he could before the inevitable moment arrived. Then he said in tones he wanted to sound natural, "Well then Ahmad, goodbye!"

I cracked. I simply felt unable to keep steady. I had never thought that I was so strongly attached to my father, that it would be so difficult for me to leave him. I looked at him in silence and felt he was about to hug me. His hands were still on my shoulders, pressing hard. He pulled himself together, and left me muttering, "Goodbye, my son."

I knew I wanted to run after him, to cling to his clothes and prevent him from leaving me.

Strangely enough, I did nothing at all! I stood still, completely still, and my voice came out meek, shaking, and resigned, "When shall I see you, father?" He stopped and turned to me, as though surprised that I hadn't grasped the reality of the situation and said,

"Indeed, you shall always see me. I shall always call! And when you're finished with your work you'll come back to the village. Oh, don't worry; there's nothing to worry about, Ahmad. The main thing is to make them happy with you and pleased with your work."

His last words seemed to come from another world, for he now moved away and soon disappeared while I stood still unable to move. I thought it was a nightmare, it couldn't happen; but what could I do? I was on my own, while my father was slipping out of my life, and Sheikh Ba Qays was still involved in his books and papers. It all took a minute or less. In fact, the whole conversation and the bargain struck between father and Ba Qays, as well as my father's departure, had all happened in the space of ten minutes. It was the longest ten minutes of my life. "Come on, boy!" the assistant said again, as though to bring me back to reality; there was no more despair, just as there was no hope.

The assistant walked up in front, never turning to look at me, as though confident that I would unquestioningly follow. I did. I tried to keep pace with his long strides, feeling more and more like a sheep being driven to a slaughterhouse.

Today, when so many years have passed and so

many strange events have taken place, I still wonder whenever I recall that situation . . . how I followed that man so easily and without thinking about what was to come. It never occurred to me to ask the assistant anything: "Who is Sheikh Salah?" "Where would I live, sleep, eat?" "With whom would I be staying?" Nothing at all seemed to occupy my mind. All I did on that day was to run on briskly behind that man with the big strides.

At last we were there--the assistant stopped at a house with a very lavish gate through which I could see some very high trees. There was a musty metal ring, which he used to knock vigorously at the door. Turning to me, he said, "This is it . . . Sheikh Salah' s house."

I had an urge to blurt out mockingly, "Really? Is it really it? Is it indeed Sheikh Salah's house? How incredible!" but didn't. The words couldn't come out, as my mind was really focused on what was behind the wall. The assistant had taken hold of the metal ring again when the door suddenly opened and an old man appeared. I did not like him. I cannot explain it but I really felt I could never love that man.

"Peace be with you, Sheikh Salah," the assistant said, saluting him.

"Peace be with you, Habrook! Well?" Sheikh Salah said.

"My master Sheikh Ba Qays sends you greetings and tells you he has found the boy you needed," Habrook quickly said. Then, pushing me by the shoulder towards Sheikh Salah, he went on, "Here he is!" Once again the urge came upon me to mock him. I wanted to say, "Is he? Well! I am the only boy standing in front of Sheikh Salah and must be 'him!'" and, once again, I held the words back and stood completely silent. I stood there, looking rather indifferent, as though they were discussing some other boy.

Sheikh Salah looked at me with the eye of an expert. I felt that he had looked in the same way at everything he acquired. I cannot, in fact, describe that look--not, as one poet has said, through "sad incompetence of human speech," but because my impressions were purely subjective. I felt like a piece of goods being offered for sale! I couldn't possibly like the man! In fact, I positively hated him, though we had known each other only for a few minutes.

"Tell Sheikh Ba Qays," Sheikh Salah said, "I am thankful and grateful! Tell him I shall see him, God willing, this evening . . . at his place!"

"I will, Sheikh Salah," the assistant said automatically, "Peace be with you!"

These words exchanged, the assistant began to walk away. He didn't look back. I looked blankly at Sheikh Salah. I wanted to feel I had human company but couldn't. My arm was suddenly pulled, and violently pressed, as Sheikh Salah pushed me under saying, "Get in." I was in agony and nearly let out a cry of pain, but I managed to control myself and follow the man into the house without a word.

I don't believe I need to explain my aversion to him. You can have a liking for a man you've just met, and feel you've known him for years; indeed, you may go on to develop a friendship, even in spite of differences in age or social position. And the opposite may happen without any justification whatsoever!

And so it fared between Sheikh Salah and me. I spent no more than three days at his house, during which I was treated as the "boy," no more, no less. He never showed any interest in me as a person--as a human being introduced into the "real world" through such an unfortunate back door. Although work at his place was never hard, I was invariably irritated whenever members of his family called me. "Boy . . ." was constantly used; sometimes I was even called by the humiliating "You there . . ."

Throughout those three days I was in the grip of severe depression. I felt so lonely that I often ignored their calls and neglected to carry out my duties. I often showed indifference and was deliberately negligent. I often moved about the house as though I was in a long nightmare, simply refusing to obey their orders.

Sheikh Salah was surprised in the beginning as though he hadn't expected the "boy" to rebel! He tried to force me to work but I was quite explicit and, at the end of three days, I made a clean breast of everything. I told him frankly that I felt miserable, desperate, lonely, frustrated, and that, in short, I didn't want to stay on. It was a strange performance because I broke down in the end and cried bitterly. I could not control myself this time, but felt extremely relieved to be able to shed tears even in the presence of my employer.

Sheikh Salah apparently didn't understand my reasons for this. He looked unwilling to accept it but then changed his mind and seemed to come to terms with the fact that I wasn't "suitable." He finally shrugged his shoulders and said indifferently, pointing at the door, "Right . . . fair enough. Get lost and never show me your face again!"

Though the words were offensive, they sounded more like a key to a prison door that I had been conscious of throughout my experience there. I sprang to my feet, wiping my tears, and shot through the door, aimlessly running through one street after another.

I don't know how I eventually found Sheikh Ba Qays's shop. Indeed, I don't know why I wanted to go to it in the first place rather than my home village! What mattered at the time was to get away from Sheikh Salah: whatever came next, I thought, couldn't be worse.

Chapter Three

Chapter Three

Bending over his books and papers, Sheikh Ba Qays became conscious of my presence as my shadow gradually lengthened in front of the shop. He lifted his head slowly, looked at me steadily but didn't appear to be surprised. My face was still wet and I was breathing fast, almost panting, as I had covered the whole distance to

his shop at a fast gallop. Quietly Sheikh Ba Qays said, "Well, what's up? Anything wrong?"

He sounded more bored than interested. I opened my mouth but couldn't say a word. I was still panting, however, when the Sheikh repeated irritably, "What's the matter? Have you lost your tongue?"

"I have . . . well . . . left Sheikh Salah's house." For a minute he was silent and his expression was definitely indignant. He put down his pen. "Left Sheikh Salah's house, did you say? But why?"

"I just left it," I said.

As though he felt a tone of flippancy in my answer, Sheikh Ba Qays roared furiously, "Just like that? You just left the service of a good family? Do you want to be homeless? Is that your father's advice?" He was now livid with rage as he went on, "You're a troublesome boy. What am I going to do with you now? What will your father say? How can I find you work when you don't want to work? Well? Answer me!"

I was silent. Then I said in a subdued voice, "I do want to work, I swear; it's just Sheikh Salah's house that I don't like."

"Really?" he shouted, "So you want to pick your employer? What is this nonsense?"

I made no answer, but just looked at him in imploring silence. The man thought for a minute, chewing his lower lip, then called to one of his assistants and said, "Go find his father. Perhaps he's still in Makkah on some business. You know where to find him."

The assistant nodded and started walking away while Sheikh Ba Qays gestured to me to sit down, still looking very upset. I sat down feeling very insecure. Would I see my father once again, whom I had lost for three long days? Would I regain my composure and overcome that feeling of being so utterly lost which had possessed me since my father left? Sheikh Ba Qays went back to work as though I didn't exist.

But father never came. The assistant came back alone. He said he couldn't find my father. Then, Sheikh Ba Qays, huffing and puffing, demanded, "Well now, what are we going to do?" With all the humility I could put in my voice, I whispered, "Whatever you say, Uncle."

"'Whatever I say?' Why? Do you listen to what I say? What I say is you go back to your master Sheikh Salah--what I say is we can do without trouble and spoilt children! Come on, there's a good boy! . . ."

"Anything but this, Uncle," I whispered, almost in tears, "Please, please!"

For a while there was no expression at all on his face, then, looking genuinely sad he said, "Well what must be done must be done . . . I really don't know what to say or what to do. However, you can spend the night at my place--tomorrow is another day."

I was overjoyed. A huge load was off my mind for I was not going back to Sheikh Salah. I rushed to Sheikh Ba Qays and kissed his hand ardently as I whispered my thanks. The man withdrew his hand

24

quickly saying, "Oh, no. May God forgive me! May God help us all!"

It now became apparent that behind his stern appearance, Sheikh Ba Qays had a heart of gold. His serious manner was only a mask and underneath it he was very kind. I thought of all this as I went with him to his place to spend my fifth night in Makkah. I did spend the night, though I couldn't sleep, as the events of the few days since I left Beni Faham had been too much for my young mind. A boy used to an uneventful and peaceful existence had suddenly been thrown into a turbulent city life mixing with different people every day. I was particularly puzzled by the contrast between the characters of Sheikh Salah and Sheikh Ba Qays; how the human heart can appear in such different guises! Why did I hate the former and like the latter? In fact, I now wished I could work at the shop or in the house of Sheikh Ba Qays, whichever was possible.

Sheikh Ba Qays took me out in the morning to the shop. I worked there all day, doing all I could to please him, obeying his orders meticulously, and doing everything I felt I should do, even without being asked. In the evening we went home together and I found it equally pleasant to serve him at his home.

Contrary to my former employer, Sheikh Ba Qays treated me as a son in his home. My duties never exceeded those of a son towards his father, so that for the first time since my father had left I stopped feeling lonely and felt I could serve Sheikh Ba Qays if he permitted. Things, however, did not turn out the way I wanted.

One day, while we were alone together at the shop, a man called. He looked particularly dignified, even though he carried a shopping bag and wore thick glasses. Sheikh Ba Qays welcomed him and invited him to sit down at his side. Their conversation showed that they were very close friends. I offered them tea, which they slowly sipped and then began to talk of personal matters--health, family, friends, acquaintances. A fragment of their conversation while I served their tea caught my attention. "By the way, Ba Qays," the man said, "couldn't you find us a boy? We need a boy to work in the house."

It was no surprise to me to hear Ba Qays tell the man, "Here he is. Why don't you try him?"
The man looked at me steadily from behind his thick glasses and said, "He looks all right to me. What's his name?"

"Ahmad . . . Ahmad bin Ayda. His father is my friend. I'm sure he'll be all right."

"I believe he'll do."

"Well then! He's all yours!"

The speed with which the bargain was struck was extraordinary. I realized that Ba Qays was not exceptionally eager to keep me at his place, and that perhaps he had put me up for a while just out of kind-ness. I was, at any rate, happy with the new man and thought I could like working in his house, contrary to what I felt towards Sheikh Salah.

Chapter Four

Chapter Four

The man rose to his feet, signaling me to follow him. I collected my things and said goodbye to Sheikh Ba Qays, thanking him for all he'd done for me. I quietly followed my new master, wondering, in terror, whether the experience of Sheikh Salah would be repeated.

It wasn't. For one thing, I

began to adjust physically and mentally to my new position as a boy in service. Also, my new master was obviously a good and easy-going man. There was a general feeling of relaxation about his home. He lived alone with a wife who was nearly his age. His wife was rather sickly and apparently weak. She, however, welcomed me and asked me to take a bath, offering me some clothes and asking her husband to buy me more. She always treated me like her own child. Her maternal feelings were really indescribable. She lavished such feelings that actually believed I was one of the family. For my part, I did all I could to live up to their expectations and carry out my duties with devotion.

For six months I lived happily, learning the tricks of the trade and getting increasingly accustomed to my new life, while the care and attention I received from that woman helped me to settle down and regain my peace of mind. As though destined for further upheavals, I was ultimately deprived of her motherly affection. She grew increasingly sick and, at the end of the six months, died. Her husband felt he could not continue to live in the house that had lost its mistress. He called me "son" before, but after her death apparently could not even speak to me. He sat quietly in his usual corner, clad in his loose cloak while his fingers played with the beads of his long rosary in obvious agitation. I kept quiet while he wrestled with wanting to tell me something, which

was not too difficult to expect, but repeatedly chang-
ing his mind.

At length, clearing his throat, and, apparently,
plucking up enough courage he said, "Listen, my son.
You know how much I like you . . ."

"Indeed! May God grant you a long life! I
could never forget what you've done for me, both
you and my late mistress! You've been everything I
had in life . . ."

"May God forgive me, my son! Thank you
anyway! We only did our duty."

We fell silent once again. I thought more than
once to save him the embarrassment and tell him that
I had guessed it all, that I didn't mind at all what he
intended to do, insofar as the circumstances were
such as they were.

"My wife, God rest her soul," he whispered as
though talking to himself, "was everything to me. We
spent a whole lifetime together, sticking together in
fair weather and foul . . . We never grumbled, but . . ."

"It's the Will of God, Uncle," I said, without
looking directly at him.

"Indeed," he again whispered, "there's no God
but Allah! No one can reverse what's preordained!"

There was silence once again. It seemed a lifetime had passed before he suddenly began to talk
again. This time, however, his words were distinct as
they raced out of his mouth, "Listen, my son! I cannot stay alone in Makkah any longer! You understand

me of course . . ."

"Naturally, Uncle!" I said, "May God grant you a long life!"

"I have a married daughter who lives in Madinah. She and her husband have asked me to move . . . to live with them in Madinah." As though relieved at having at last broken the news to me, he simply looked at me hopefully. He obviously expected me to guess what he was driving at, more or less implicitly.

"But of course, Uncle!" I said with real feeling, "God be with you! I do understand--May God help you!"

"What about you? What are you going to do?"

"Oh, I have faith in God! Oh, Uncle, please don't worry about me!" I said.

"Thank you, my son!" He closed his eyes in obvious satisfaction with my quick response, then whispered again, "Thanks be to God! You're a good boy, my son!"

"Thank you, Uncle! You and your late wife always treated me well!"

"Thanks be to God!"

He rose to his feet, hugged me affectionately and said, "I needn't remind you I'd like you to keep in touch! I shall give you my address in Madinah; I hope that your news will always be good!"

The tone of finality put an end to our conversation. Once again I was on my own, faced to ponder my future and what I should do to secure it. Naturally, my thoughts immediately turned to Sheikh Ba Qays.

Chapter Five

Chapter Five

Sheikh Ba Qays warmly received me. His reserved manner was replaced by a genuine welcome, which I attributed to my satisfactory performance during the long period I spent at that good man's house. He ordered tea and asked me to sit by his side, showing undivided attention to me, then said, "Well, well, well!

You seem to have grown up so much in these months!" I was too shy to reply, and he went on to say, "I know all about it! I know why you're here! The man has told me; he's been actually singing your praises!" Shaking his head in obvious sorrow, he added, "His wife, God rest her soul, was a good woman, in the full sense of the word! It's the Will of God; no one can reverse it!"

Realizing that I would be embarrassed to disturb him once again with my "work problems," he went on to say, "You don't have to worry about work! I've got an 'uncle' for you who's the best you could find! His name is Sheikh Abdul-Hamid--do you know him?"

"You're the only person I know in Makkah."

"Not to worry! He's a good man, a very good man. He's been looking for a boy for some time now! I would've recommended you to him before now, if I didn't know you were happy at your old uncle's!"

"I wish I knew how to return your favors, Uncle Ba Qays!"

"What's this you're saying, Son? You're my responsibility! I am only doing my duty . . . God willing!"

"Thank you, Uncle!" I said as I rose, having finished my tea, and in a straightforward but businesslike manner (which I daresay I had acquired from experience) asked, "What is his address?"

"Who? Sheikh Abdul-Hamid?"

"Yes! My new uncle!"

35

"I'm glad to see you're taking your work seriously, young though you are! You have grown up, haven't you, in the past few months!" Indeed, I was soon walking briskly towards my new uncle's house. With the benefit of hindsight I could say I was in effect taking my first steps not to a house but to a new way of life! It was the beginning of the change that made me what I am today, having started as a boy in service. The details of the events of that day, though quite ordinary in the beginning, remain indelibly in my mind.

Sheikh Abdul-Hamid's house was quite big: from the outside it looked more like a small palace. It was a perfect specimen of the traditional Arab mansion with imposing gates and a vast orchard. I could even hear birds singing inside as I approached to knock on the door. A strange feeling of peace overcame me and, when the door was opened, Sheikh Abdul-Hamid's welcome made me feel really at home. I instantly moved about freely as though I had lived there before, enjoying the spacious rooms and the long and labyrinthine corridors, especially the central one that led to the garden. For a while I looked at the pool in the middle, feeling that the birds I had heard were actually members of the family. They too moved about freely and perched on the various pieces of furniture, which were comfortable and in good taste, though not excessively luxurious.

As the days passed, the house became home, and I grew increasingly familiar with life in it. I was particularly pleased to find I had a playmate--a girl, a little younger than myself, but who was willing to share the childish games I enjoyed most. Perhaps the lack of a playmate had accounted for my looking so "grown up" as Sheikh Ba Qays had observed; now I was myself again, and emphatically acting my "real age"!

While members of the family accepted me as a matter of course (that is, as they were wont to accept a new boy to run their errands and help them about the house), I felt that a whole new world had opened to me. The feeling that I was at home, that I had a playmate, was no doubt behind this. There was, however, another reason, perhaps more important--Aziza!

Aziza was my playmate's name. She was always well dressed (though never showy or gaudy), always held her head high and let her hair down! I was particularly attracted to her long hair, and when the time came for me to read poetry, I realized why poets compared a girl's hair to the rays of the sun, waterfalls and moonbeams! It was on my very first day that her frivolous tone, so childishly charming, brought me alive . . . rather the child that was in me! Even as I introduced myself to Sheikh Abdul-Hamid, Aziza rushed to me making beautiful noises and abruptly said, "Come on! Let's play!"

I naturally made no answer. Sheikh Abdul-Hamid, however, responded to her words with a guffaw, saying, "This is Ahmad, our new boy. He is here to work, I hope, not to play."

At her age she did not know the difference between work and play, and this made her go on insisting that I should play with her. Who knows? Perhaps she too, being the only child in the household, was feeling lonely. Loneliness affects people in the same way, be they masters who give orders or servants who obey them.

With the laugh still lingering on his lips, Sheikh Abdul-Hamid turned to me and explained, "This is typical of Aziza, she is always like this . . . strong headed . . . she must always have her way. Go on my son . . . go on and play with her a little . . . it can't be helped . . . consider you have started your duties as from now."

As if I was not still a mere child fond of playing! As if I had forgotten my childhood in Beni Faham, where life had been a continuous round of games and merry-making! Sometimes we invented our own games, which were inspired by our immediate environment, and sometimes we copied games played in other villages. The times our parents had to go out looking for us in the dark of night! We would become so absorbed in our play that time, the merging of day into night, did not exist for us!

My new working life, it is true, had put a barrier between me and the pastimes of childhood. It had not, however, altered the fact that I was still a child who had not had his full share of them. Here at least I was offered a chance of being a child once more. Indeed, I was ordered by my master to do so. There was nothing to do but obey . . . my own childish longings and my master's order in the bargain! And who was I to have for a playmate? Aziza . . . of all people . . . Aziza!

I soon discovered that Aziza was different from my playmates in the village. She was a child, like all the children I knew before--like my brothers and sisters, my friends or the little girls next door. But she was radiantly beautiful, and exceedingly courteous . . . her actions were characterized by a kind of natural pride that she had acquired from her upbringing in a distinguished environment.

There was another difference too. In the village, I treated my playmates as equals--our background was the same. It was not, naturally, like this with Aziza... She was the daughter of my master, and I was a mere "boy" that had come to serve in her house. Playing with her was a duty--a kind of "work"--since I was ordered to do it by my master.

These considerations, however, both positive and negative, did not stop me from enjoying playing with Aziza and trying by all means to amuse her and make her laugh. I soon became Aziza's favorite playmate. And, in spite of her tender years, she paid me, in return, a lot of attention and literally showered me with her kindness.

Every time her father bought her sweets she wouldn't have any until I had some. She had a quaint way, too, of handing me my share: she would unexpectedly shoot them at me, hitting me in the face or on the head. This used to make her laugh a lot. Gradually, however, I became more skilled in avoiding her shots and either would succeed in catching the missile or avoiding it by a quick movement of the head. Invariably, Aziza laughed and her sweet eyes shone with happiness. This glow made me happy too, and the memory of it has remained with me ever since.

Chapter Six

Chapter Six

The truth is that in the household of Sheikh Abdul-Hamid I was never treated as a mere "boy." Everybody--the master, the mistress and their daughter--looked upon me as one of the family. This made me anxious to do everything to please them and make them feel their trust and love were not misplaced.

My loneliness, my sense of loss and of being lost fell away from me. I was once again a child enjoying a comfortable life, contented and secure. This made me, I am ashamed to confess, nearly forget my family and my village--all that had made up my former world . . . a world I thought I couldn't exchange for anything else.

I never lacked anything, and therefore, saved up all my pay. Indeed, I once begged Sheikh Abdul-Hamid as he was handing me the money not to do so. I felt that his kindness to me was more than enough to pay for my service. To take money from him as well seemed to me like ingratitude. Sheikh Abdul-Hamid, however, would not hear of it. Giving me my 30 riyals he said, "Take them my son . . . I know all about the difficult circumstances that forced you into service . . . Sheikh Ba Qays told me everything . . . I do not regard this sum as a salary I pay you. It is a gift from a father to his son." I was so moved by his words that I cried. Taking the money, I said, "God grant you a long life, Uncle. May we never lose you!"

Life went on peacefully for the next six months free of trouble and worry. I often wondered in my mind how people can be so similar outwardly and yet so different in character and temperament. How vastly different, for instance, was Sheikh Abdul-Hamid from Sheikh Salah! The former dedicated himself to good deeds and charitable acts. Consequently, he enjoyed an excellent reputation and a good name that never failed to evoke love, respect and praise whenever mentioned. The latter lived for himself alone, and was so wrapped up in himself that it never occurred to him that the "boy" he made suffer was a human being who had hopes and dreams, who could feel happiness and sorrow.

This riddle intrigued me for a long time and finally proved too difficult for my young mind to tackle, nor was I too worried about not finding a solution or an explanation. I was too absorbed in my daily happiness in the household of Sheikh Abdul-Hamid.

One fine day my father arrived. A long time had passed since we had parted. He embraced me warmly, the tears streaming down his cheeks, and said, his voice tremulous as he pressed me repeatedly to his chest, "Allah be praised... Allah be praised... How you've grown! You're a big boy now... a man!" We sat down and talked... talked of everything. Seeing Father again awakened all my old memories of the village. It was as if his face and eyes reflected images of the past I had thought I could slough off--a past I nearly forgot. It all came back to me in Father's voice as he talked after a whole year of separation.

He rounded off his stream of words by asking, "And now, you tell me all that's happened to you since I last saw you." I related all. I also told him of my happiness in my new situation at Abdul-Hamid's household, and described at length how well that family treated me. Smiling, as if he could guess my reply, my father asked, "In all this time, you haven't tried to visit us even once?" Smiling back I replied, "I was afraid to . . . I am so attached to the village and everything there that I thought if I went I'd never be able to go away again. That would have been against your will, since you brought me here to work and meant for me to stay."

My final words brought something into my mind. I got up at once and went to a corner of my room, which stood at one side of the garden, opened a small box and extracted a small, carefully wrapped cloth purse. I placed it in my father's hand saying, "Take this Father. I have kept it for you all this time. It's all there!"

My father opened it. It contained a large sum of money in different denominations--one hundred, fifty, ten, and five riyal notes, apart from coins. My father's surprise was only too obvious; he simply muttered, "What's this son? What is it?" I quickly said, "My earnings, Father! It's all I have earned since I started work. It must be well over fifteen hundred. Sheikh Abdul-Hamid is a very generous man, and his wife no less generous. You know, Father, they always give me a little something now and again, as though my high wages weren't enough!"

Father fell silent for a moment, then almost inaudibly said, "Bless them, bless you, my son, but . . . this is too much!"

"Oh, no! It's all yours, Father! Take it all! I have no need of it while I stay here; indeed, I shall be getting more and more!"

"You might! You just might! I must leave you something . . . "

"I don't think it'll be of use to me! I am fully provided for at this place . . . food, drink, clothes-- everything!"

"Bless you my son! Bless you indeed! You have actually saved me from a real crisis. Bless you Ahmad!"

As though coming into reality at last, my father accepted the money and hugged me with genuine feeling, saying, "You've become a man, my son! You're earning your own living!"

A few months later my father called again, and was welcomed by Sheikh Abdul-Hamid with equal warmth. He made a habit, in fact, of calling every few months and was always accorded the same hospitality and welcome. Time passed as though it was an interrupted holiday, until one day when I was summoned to see Sheikh Abdul-Hamid.

Chapter
Seven

Chapter Seven

Looking serious and almost grim, Sheikh Abdul-Hamid signaled me to sit nearby. I did. I was a little worried as I recalled a similar situation when the relationship with my previous employer came to an end, but then, I thought, it was different this time. I had expected that "end" ever since my previous

employer's wife died and there was nothing at all to suggest this now--not even remotely--and yet I felt uneasy. What could Sheikh Abdul-Hamid possibly want from me?

Fear clutched my heart in a cold steely grip as I sat silently near him. My heart thumped as my eyes hung upon the lips that had remained unparsed since my arrival. What was it? I wondered. He still remained silent, and I felt with growing certainty that what he had to tell me was something very unpleasant.

"Listen Ahmad," he said at last, "You know, I want you to start moving in the right direction."

"There's nothing I complain of, Uncle. I am in the right direction, thanks to God Almighty and to your care and kindness."

"Listen son, and stop interrupting. I haven't called you here so that we may exchange compliments!"

I held my tongue. I was by then completely baffled as to his purpose in calling me. Had he wanted to sack me or impart some bad news he wouldn't have adopted such an affable, cordial manner. Besides, what could he mean by that "right direction" in which he wanted me to move? Move! But I was quite all right where I was!

My thoughts were interrupted when Sheikh Abdul-Hamid took up a folded piece of paper and handed it to me saying, "Read this, if you please."

My hand trembled as I took the paper. My distracted eyes tripped over the lines as I wondered why he should make such a request of me when he knew perfectly well that I could neither read nor write! Was he simply poking fun at me? A wave of scathing shame engulfed me as I gazed and gazed at the piece of paper. To me it meant nothing but an unintelligible jumble of lines, figures, and dots. I quietly placed the paper in my lap and said, bending my head in humiliation, "I . . . I can't read. But I can read parts of the Qur'an," I added eagerly.

"This may be true. All the same, I am sure that in reading those parts of the Qur'an you depend more on your memory than on your knowledge of the alphabet. Am I right?"

"Yes, you're right," I whispered, shame choking me. As he watched me in silence, I started reproaching myself bitterly: why had I neglected this matter so completely? Why was it that I had never tried to learn to read in all this time? Why hadn't I asked for help--from Aziza, for instance? If she had taught me one letter a day, even one in a week or a month, I would have been able to read by now and I would have saved myself this terrible embarrassment!

My angry thoughts were interrupted by the sheikh's voice. He smiled at me as he said, "You see? I was right." My head still bent I murmured, "Yes Uncle."

"Then I can tell you, my son, that I only called

you to ask you to start a new phase in your life, a phase in which you can receive education like other boys of your age."

"Education? But how? You know how it is, Uncle."

"I know . . . I know . . . Your work here takes up all your mornings. But there are night schools. You can join one. They were created for people like you whose mornings are busy."

My heart leapt up with joy. The good sheikh, God reward him, had pondered my dilemma, and had come up with a solution. He went on, "I shall help you join one of the night schools nearby. I want you to get a reasonable level of education, as it is unthinkable for you to spend the rest of your life as a domestic servant. To be absolutely honest, I feel it would shame me to have an illiterate live in my house when I am such a learned man. How can I go on teaching at the Grand Mosque when a man so near to my heart has no access to knowledge? It's simply wrong!"

"You're right, Uncle!"

"I'd like to give you education... and be rewarded by God for it." Though pleased by the sheikh's words, I asked him almost unconsciously, "But shouldn't I ask my father's permission first?"

"Certainly," answered the sheikh smiling, "It's good of you to think of this, but I'm sure your father won't say 'no'!"

I rose up, took leave of the sheikh and went to

my room where I sat, practically stunned by what I had heard. The words of that good man held a strange sort of promise which I had to consider. Sheikh Abdul-Hamid's words, his interest in my problem, and his proposed "action" opened my eyes to a number of facts which I ought to have seen for myself a long time ago. On the one hand I felt ashamed to realize that I had not as yet considered a "career" but that I had lived as though I meant to remain a servant all my life, as he put it. And on the other hand, I was deeply moved by the extent to which Sheikh Abdul-Hamid was eager to help me. Busy as he was and quite taken up by his private affairs, he still could find time to worry over the future of mere hireling in his household.

He had found the means to advance me in life and opened up for me new vistas of hope.

Indeed, I have learned ever since that was the true, if not the only, measure of a man. To really care for and busy himself over the affairs of a lowly person, no matter how insignificant in the general scheme of humanity, is the true mark of superiority of soul and magnitude of spirit. This may be why we are always touched and moved by the simple humane actions of great men, whether we actually witness them or only read about them. A truly great man can always find time and energy to expend on those who are less fortunate than himself and, therefore, are in real need of his help and assistance.

The image of Aziza floated into my mind suddenly interrupting this stream of thoughts. I had given her all the simple innocent affection--I wouldn't say "love"--which an eleven-year-old was capable of and she had returned it. I had become aware of this mutual bond between Aziza and myself. At that time it looked no more than a mere childish attachment unworthy of real notice. Nevertheless, it was, in fact, the kind of attachment that left indelible traces on the soul.

Aziza? What about Aziza?

Up till then it had never occurred to me that I could not aspire to her--being a mere houseboy in her father's employ, and an ignorant and illiterate one at that. A boy who could boast no more than a meager smattering of learning received at the hands of the village sheikh and consisting merely of knowledge of a few short verses of the Qur'an. Furthermore, it was a knowledge that relied rather on the ability to memorize than to decipher the shapes and sounds of the alphabet!

I had no definite idea as to the future of our relationship. I vaguely realized, however, the change that education could effect in my social standing, the new scope it could give me. To pursue this end was the least I could do to be worthy of her, or at least worthy of entertaining the mere dream, thought, or memory of her.

My father, when consulted, was enthusiastically

in favor of the project. The sheikh made all the arrangements and I joined a night school. The household buzzed with the news: this crucial step became the central if not the sole topic of conversation.

Chapter
Eight

Chapter Eight

I was the youngest in the class. The scene that greeted my eyes upon first stepping into the classroom, in great apprehension, was strange and unexpected. Ranged in the seats, in rows according to their years, were fifteen men aged between twenty-five and sixty-five. Young men at the dawn of life and white-bearded old men on the threshold of decrepitude were united in the pursuit of learning, having at last found the means and opportunity.

As my eyes roved over my new colleagues they stopped at one particular elderly man who attracted my attention. He looked so attentive, so energetic; he responded so readily to the teacher's instructions, answering questions and writing laboriously, yet with such determination, on his black slate that one could not help respecting him. We called him "Uncle Mahmoud." I admired that man profoundly; his example fired my enthusiasm and nourished my energy and perseverance. If such an old man, I thought, who could not be very far off from the grave (though of course life and death are solely determined by God's will), could still hope to learn, what was there that an eleven-year-old boy like myself could not aspire to? A favorite saying of Sheikh Abdul-Hamid crossed my mind. He used to say, nodding his head affirmatively, "You are as young as you feel."

Armed with such determination, I launched into my new life, exerting myself in both study and work. Sheikh Abdul-Hamid followed my progress with the serious interest of a father. Nor was Aziza less interested and caring: she questioned me closely about my daily lessons, made fun of my mistakes, corrected them and urged me do to more and better.

Time flowed on . . .

I covered several stages of my education in a

very short time and I was able to catch up with boys of my own age and get my general primary education certificate in only three years, thus making up for lost time. The day the results were announced and we found that I had, with the grace of God, succeeded, the jubilation in our household was beyond description. Before I had time to think of what to do next I found that, as usual, Sheikh Abdul Hamid had anticipated my thoughts. Shortly afterwards he summoned me and said, "Listen Ahmad . . . I think you realize that the situation has changed a great deal?"

Not knowing exactly what he meant I replied naively, "Certainly, Uncle. I can now read and write, and do sums as well."

"That is not exactly what I meant, my boy," he said, smiling kindly. "What I am thinking of is . . . 'What next?'"

"Next?"

"Yes. High school, of course."

"High school!" I echoed in amazement.

"Indeed, or hadn't it occurred to you? Hadn't you thought of going further with your education?"

"A full-time job. That's what you mean, isn't it?"

"That's right. This is exactly what I wanted to discuss with you."

"God grant you a long life, Sir. You've already showered me with your favors . . ."

"God forgive me my sins. I am only serving God in this and my reward lies with Him."

58

"From now on," he continued after pausing a while, "you will study by day and do your house jobs in the evening."

"But that's impossible, Uncle. My mistress needs me in the daytime. You are at work then, and Aziza is away at school, and . . ."

"Don't worry about your mistress. It's all settled," he interrupted with a smile. "Nanny Gom'a will be coming to us regularly every day to stay the mornings while you're away at school."

"Nanny Gom'a! Who's she?"

"A former bond slave who, with the grace of God, has been freed. She still works, though. She knows us well and has always loved your mistress. See now? Everything has been arranged to everybody's satisfaction."

Words failed me. I did not know how to express to this man what I felt about him and all he had done for me. He seemed to me larger than life. What I admired most about him was his decisive way of settling matters. Once an idea took root in his mind, he immediately inspected all its possible angles and then took the necessary measures to surmount any anticipated obstacles and forestall any eventualities, so that when he proposed it came as a definite and complete plan of action.

It was thus that Nanny Gom'a came into our lives. She instantly drew everybody's affection to her--mine more than anybody else's. Maybe because her presence meant that I could devote more time to my studies, but also because of her gentle, motherly tenderness and the keen interest she took in all my affairs.

I poured all my energies into my high school studies, always spurred on by the thought that I must not fail those who entertained such high hopes of me. I was also encouraged by my desire to better myself and cultivate those seeds of ambition that Sheikh Abdul-Hamid had first planted in me. There was Aziza too! She figured as a major part of that ambition!

Aziza? But who are you? What are you to aspire to Aziza?! Your little mistress! The daughter of your master! Though at the core of my determination to better myself was that nebulous passion, the feeling never did, perhaps never dared to, articulate itself as a real hope of ever one day making Aziza mine. I had the urge, the drive to be somebody, yet felt that no matter how far I got I would never make a suitable husband for her or she a fitting wife for me. I would always remain first and last a houseboy . . . a mere servant. I belonged downstairs, in the servants' quarters. The lowly hand of the servant would remain forever stretched out to receive from the superior hands of the masters. Mine would always remain the humble lowly hand, no matter what I did or how high I climbed in life. I had to school myself into never raising my eyes above my base station in life.

I even went so far in self-abasement as to think of my pure and innocent feelings as downright sinful.

I felt I was wronging those who took me into their home and gave me everything, including an education. I told myself that it was my duty never to betray their dignity and high standing. The only honorable thing to do was to bury my passion so deep that no one would ever discover it, or ever suspect that I regarded Aziza as anything other than a superior and gracious mistress.

It was true, I argued with myself, that I had always been treated as a member of the family; ever since I came they had insisted on my sitting at the table with them and would even keep food waiting for me--unusual treatment for a servant! It was true, I still debated, that Sheikh Abdul-Hamid and his wife adopted exactly the same manner towards me as with Aziza with not the slightest distinction. Nevertheless, I should not take advantage of their generosity and turn it into an excuse for jumping the bounds of my menial station, or for allowing my feelings to soar so high as to trespass upon their superior regions by entertaining the hope of marrying her!

I was equally determined to complete my secondary education as I was resolved to curb my feelings or, at least, suppress them. I was especially careful to avoid hurting Aziza by looking in any improper or suggestive manner at her; I was determined to keep my feelings in the dark.

My attempt at suppressing my feelings developed into a daily conflict, an integral part of my battle for survival--at study or at work. A time came when

I felt embarrassed whenever our eyes met: I had to look away while she, observing my deliberate effort, simply smiled. So innocent and pure, she could not understand my embarrassment, and apparently interpreted it as a sign of being tired or overworked.

The truth is, embarrassing as they were, her looks had always been "neutral"; never did I feel that she harbored anything comparable to my passion. She was nevertheless interested, perhaps immoderately so, in my progress. She always encouraged me, egged me on to read other advanced books, and often lent me some of the books she had already read at school. A life of struggle, involving work and study and an incessant effort to suppress my feelings came to an end, temporarily, when I obtained my secondary school certificate.

On the last day of the exams, I remember, I went back to the house, well pleased with myself, to tell Uncle Sheikh Abdul-Hamid that I had done well and that I hoped to pass, God willing. It was the beginning of the summer, and it was the custom of the family to move to Ta'if for the whole season. So we started packing. Our preparations completed, we loaded our luggage into the car and Sheikh Abdul-Hamid took the driver's seat. My mistress settled herself in the middle of the back seat with Aziza on her right and myself on the left.

The car sped along the road from Makkah to Ta'if. We were silent, each preoccupied with his own private thoughts. Meanwhile, the car radio droned on unnoticed. Suddenly, there was an announcement: the results of the school certificate exams would be read out shortly. At once we were all ears. My body stiffened in expectation and grew pale. We exchanged furtive glances that spoke eloquently of our tense expectancy.

Without turning his head, Sheikh Abdul-Hamid said encouragingly, as he managed a difficult twist of the road, "There you are, Ahmad. Now you'll know." With touching warmth, my mistress answered, "He'll pass, God willing. I'm sure he'll make it." As for Aziza, she only smiled at me reassuringly. When she noticed how pale I was she said calmly, "Don't be such a coward. We know how hard you've studied and you know you did reasonably well on the exam. Why should you worry then?" I made no reply; only my loud gulps indicated the depth of my trepidation.

We listened attentively as the announcer read out the names. Every time the name Ahmad was mentioned we were startled and I felt my heart jump into my throat, only to relax at discovering that it wasn't me after all. Then came a pause . . . an interminable one I thought. A veil of despair closed over me. We exchanged glances as it began to dawn upon us that perhaps I hadn't made it. Aziza seemed to partake of my bitter disappointment. All the hopes I had cherished were suddenly dashed.

Nothing was said, but our silence was more eloquent than any words. I was beginning to sink into a kind of stupor when suddenly the announcer's voice burst upon our ears: "We now continue our broadcast of the School Certificate Results." My uncle heaved a huge sigh of relief and said with a laugh, addressing the announcer, "May God forgive you! You frightened the life out of us!"

"He did indeed," agreed my mistress, shaking her head disapprovingly and adding, "He gave us such a fright. I thought they had come to the end of the successful lists."

"Announcers usually take turns reading long items, or have you forgotten?" reminded Aziza, laughing in apparent relief.

"Let's hope for the best, my daughter," murmured my uncle hopefully, "Let's hope for the best."

I however made no comment. The shock I had suffered had rendered me utterly indifferent and inert. I hardly listened as the announcer went on and on with his endless list of names--the list that did not include the name "Ahmad bin Ayda." I suddenly wanted to scream, to beg Sheikh Abdul-Hamid to switch off the radio. My nerves were frayed to shreds. I felt I could no longer bear to hear the name Ahmad followed by a surname other than mine. I felt certain I had failed . . . I had failed everyone.

"Ahmad bin Ayda."

The announcer said those words in the same monotonous tones, unaware of the turmoil his simple utterance had caused in our car as it rolled fast on its way to Ta'if.

"It's my name . . . it's my name!" I shouted. "Allah be praised!" I yelled uncontrollably, my voice overflowing with joy and emotion. They all laughed and the oppressive sense of despair that hung upon the car was transformed into a frenzy of joy. Words of congratulations flew about the car . . .

"Congratulations Ahmad!" "God bless you my boy!"

" . . . Congratulations Ahmad!" Aziza tailed out the chorus, real joy dancing in her beautiful eyes, "A thousand congratulations!" Before I knew what I was doing, I clutched Sheikh Abdul-Hamid's head and started kissing him. My mistress held me in her arms and kissed my head with the gentleness of a tender and loving mother. I took Aziza's hand in mine and pressed warmly. Suddenly I realized what I was doing and quickly withdrew my hand. I was embarrassed and ashamed and began to reproach myself for this lapse. My only consolation was that my foolishness had stopped at that.

Aziza had blushed deeply. I bent my head feeling more and more embarrassed. It was the first time I had held her hand in this manner. I suddenly felt weak. My mistress, who had observed me, made no comment. I tried to read her reaction to what had occurred, and was relieved to find that she regarded the whole incident as perfectly natural in the circumstances.

Sensing my painful embarrassment, Aziza stretched her hand across her mother's lap and held my cold hand. She pressed it and whispered gently, "Once more, congratulations, Ahmad . . . A thousand congratulations."

I tried to say something but the words stuck in my throat. For the rest of the journey I was silent and failed to take in anything of what was being said about my success. We reached our house in Ta'if. The luggage was unloaded and we began our summer holidays.

Chapter Nine

Chapter Nine

Sleep eluded me that night. I lay down, my eyes wide open and my arms folded under my head, and gazed at the moon. She had spread her mantle of silver over the whole roof, dispelling the darkness of the night.

Sleeplessness was very natural and expected on a night like this: it had witnessed the crowning

of my efforts with success and marked the beginning of a new stage in my life. All this, however--my success, the school certificate, the thought of the future and the intricate filigree of extravagant dreams traced by hope and ambition--all this did not account for my sleeplessness. Lying there on the roof, so still, my eyes fixed on the full moon, my mind was possessed solely by the thought of Aziza. I went over how I had dared hold her hand in both mine and press it-- how, in a moment, I had completely forgotten all the barriers that stood between us. It had been sheer madness. It was unpardonable! My tumult of joy was no excuse. How did I dare? How could I?! My inferior hand had gripped hers in a fraternal gesture that was only acknowledged among equals. "I am only a servant . . . just a servant . . . nothing but a servant," I repeated to myself over and over. The words raged and stormed inside my head so loudly that I almost feared the din would wake up the slumbering town. I even lifted my head a little and looked around gingerly. All was quiet. I sighed in relief and resumed my former position.

Silence reigned except for the intermittent song of the cricket and occasional croaking of the frog--the familiar, well-remembered sounds that formed the symphony of summer in country places. I grappled once more with my thoughts. All day I had tried hard to find a chance to talk to Aziza alone. I had badly wanted to apologize, to explain that I had meant no disrespect, that what had happened had been a mistake, an impulse of high spirits triggered off by the sudden shock of joy. I had wanted to reassure her that I never meant to go beyond my limits.

I had gotten her alone at last. It happened as I was carrying her luggage to her room. She followed me in and showed me where to put the bags. I made for the door, but stopped short before reaching it. Aziza was surprised in a normal innocent manner that did not spell either anger or aversion.

"Is there anything?" I bent my head and made no answer.

"What is it, Ahmad? Is there anything wrong? Tell me."

I could see she was beginning to get worried. She thought that either I was sick or there was something terribly wrong.

"It's nothing little Mistress, God be praised . . . Only . . ."

"Only what? Speak."

Flushing with embarrassment, my ears nearly burning, I drew nearer and, my eyes fixed on the floor, faltered out, "It's only that I wanted to . . . to apologize."

"Apologize?! For what?"

"For what I did today."

"And what was it you did today?"

Now it was my turn to be surprised. I looked up at her as I explained in confusion, "I mean what I did in the car . . . holding your hand . . . you know . . . and . . ."

"Oh, that! I see. You know you really worried me there! Honestly! I thought it was something serious." As she said this, she laughed in her usual childish carefree manner.

A terrible weight slipped off my shoulders. Encouraged by her attitude I had added warmly, "I swear to you, I never meant any disrespect. I swear it. It was only that I felt . . ."

"What was the harm?" she interrupted with a smile. "Don't worry about it anymore, Ahmad. What counts is the intention, not the deed, as you well know. People are taken to task over their intentions, isn't that so? I know that you regard me as a sister, Ahmad, so you don't have to worry."

A sister?!

This meeting stood out sharply among the events of the day as I reviewed them, lying there in the moonlight. She had behaved towards me in the same cordial, innocent way I was familiar with. She had taken my impulsive action to mean nothing but the expression of fraternal affection. I should have felt relieved at this, of course, since I had meant to keep my passion for her a hidden secret. Strangely enough, I wasn't. I was rather upset and irritated.

Her reaction could only mean one thing, I told myself. She looked upon me as a brother, nothing more. A brother?! When I could feel my heart bursting with the force of my passion and the pressure of secrecy! A brother? When I wanted to scream out my love for the entire world to hear!

Her feelings were understandable, I thought. She regarded me as lower than herself. She, being superior, could only understand our mutual affection as part of masters and servants. Was that everything then? I felt so downhearted, so utterly miserable. I told myself I had to stop trying to better myself. I had to recognize and accept my humble station in life, my identity as a servant. I feared that if I did not become reconciled with my situation, other rash deeds would follow which were bound to reveal my burning secret.

I turned over and lay on my side. Having made that decision in my arduous soul-searching, I tried to go to sleep. At that moment, the sweet dawn prayer calls floated up from the minarets of Ta'if. The sweetness moved me to tears. They flowed, bathing my face. I did not try to stop them. It was as if my heart itself, in its anguished frustration, was seeking relief in weeping. The tears flowed on in silence as I continued to raise my eyes to the moon, which had now sheltered behind a cloud.

Among my duties in Ta'if was to prepare a suitable reception area in one corner of the garden for Sheikh Abdul-Hamid's guests. They were mostly high government officials and wealthy celebrities who were either permanent dwellers of the town or seasonal visitors like us.

I had to look after the guests, prepare and serve hookahs and tea, fruit and sweets, and generally remain at their beck and call. They, naturally, got to know me well and treated me with the same courtesy that Sheikh Abdul-Hamid showed me.

I found myself the topic of conversation on more than one occasion. The sheikh, of course, had told them all about me and had held forth about my determination and perseverance. He told them how I had made good in my studies and was able to obtain three certificates in a short period, which indicated, he was wont to say, that I had a natural aptitude for scholarship.

Regularly, whenever Sheikh Abdul-Hamid reached that point in his speech, everybody turned round and offered me their congratulations and best wishes for the future. I, naturally, would answer by praising God for my success and for having guided my steps to the shelter of Sheikh Abdul Hamid's kindness. I would add that, after Allah of course, I owed everything to the sheikh's generosity.

One day, a high official in the education sector, by the name of Abdul-Razik, said to my uncle, "I think you will agree with me, Brother Abdul-Hamid, that one must never leave a job unfinished." A little mystified, my uncle asked, "What do you mean, Brother Abdul-Razik?"

"This young man here--by the grace of God, you have helped him this far in his education. I do think you ought to take him the whole way."

"The whole way?"

"Yes. Why don't you send him to a university?"

University?! The word rang out in my ears with such loud repercussions it made my head swim. I, Ahmad bin Ayda, the house-boy, the base menial--I go to a university? University?!

But how could it be accomplished? I was destitute,

penniless. The country hadn't then started to build the flourishing university education it boasts now. The fruits of that awakening were destined for subsequent generations, not mine. Nowadays, there are universities all over the country, offering free education of the highest level in all branches of knowledge. It was different in my time. In my day, if a Saudi boy wanted a university degree he had to seek it abroad, usually in Egypt. Expensive government scholarships were available, of course, but on a very limited scale, since the country then had meager resources and heavy commitments.

University! How could I afford it? My wages were regularly sent home to help my family. Mr. Abdul-Razik was indulging in daydreams or definitely joking. To a boy like me, a university education was as far away and unreachable as the skies. I was extremely surprised, therefore, when I heard Sheikh Abdul-Hamid's reply to Mr. Abdul-Razik's proposal. "Believe me Abdul-Razik, I had the same idea," he said. "I think you can help us here. If you assist Ahmad in obtaining a government scholarship, I will willingly undertake to meet whatever other expenses he may need for travelling. The study program, as you know, has to be arranged at your end."

My heart beat fast. I heard them talking about me, discussing the question of sending me abroad to study as if I was a cherished cause. I heard them all supporting the idea, agreeing with the scholarship, which was Mr. Abdul-Razik's responsibility and duty, since he, himself, had proposed the project.

"In truth, Mr. Abdul-Razik," said one of the guests, "If this thing is to come off, it'll have to come through your efforts."

"God willing, God willing,' said Mr. Abdul-Razik, laughing. "Look Ahmad, bring all your papers to my office in Jeddah and I'll see what can be done."

"A thousand thanks to you, sir,' I said, joy rioting in my chest and my heart leaping high, "A thousand thanks." Once more I was destined to keep a solitary vigil, with only the moon and my feverish thoughts to keep me company. The word "university" dominated my consciousness as I went over the events of the day, recalling the momentous conversation between Sheikh Abdul-Hamid and Mr. Abdul-Razik, and the unanimous approval with which the suggestion was met. Though it had never crossed my mind, everyone had seemed to find it quite reasonable and plausible.

University! Was it really possible? Could it really be that the houseboy Ahmad bin Ayda, who was in the employ of Sheikh Abdul-Hamid and had served others before, would become a university student? Would he have access to the limitless horizons such a course of action offered in a man's life, putting it in a totally new direction? I wondered then whether God had chosen, so many years ago, to place me with Sheikh Abdul-Hamid so that one day I would be that fortunate boy, holding a secondary school certificate and opening the door to university life. If He hadn't done so, would I be where I was now?

God had decreed and supplied the means of realizing His design. Why then should I bother myself with so many speculations? In my thoughts Aziza became linked with my university prospect. I could not dissociate them. They meant one and the same thing. Would my university degree give me sanction to hope for Aziza? I curbed my thoughts. I had long ago decided to suppress my feelings and stay within the legitimate boundaries of my class. A university education was one thing, I said to myself, and Aziza was another. They are two separate issues I should never confuse. I must not allow my passion to mislead me. Having reached that conclusion, I forced my eyes shut and made myself sleep. Two words, however, still hovered persistently over my consciousness: "Aziza" and "university."

Sheikh Abdul-Hamid said, in his typically kind and interested manner, "Ahmad, I think that you should settle your affairs quickly. You yourself should follow up your interests. I don't want you to waste your energy on anything else. Forget about your work here now and concentrate on the scholarship."

I was deeply touched and stammered, "But . . . Uncle . . ."

"Do as I say. It's no easy matter; it's a university scholarship you're after," he interrupted firmly. "It wouldn't hurt the household to be without you for a while, while you complete the procedures."

Chapter Ten

Chapter Ten

The scholarship became my sole preoccupation. It involved a lot of coming and going between Makkah, Jeddah and Ta'if, obtaining documents and filling out forms. Mr. Abdul-Razik proved true to his word and did all he could to help. My high grades and excellent school record worked in my favor and helped to push my

name up on the list of candidates. My efforts were finally crowned with success and, by the grace of God, I was nominated for a scholarship. I was to go to Egypt. It only remained for me to complete my preparations for departure.

Typically, Sheikh Abdul-Hamid paid close attention to the minute details of the project. He had interested himself in every step of the way and had used his influence and whatever connections he had to help me. Once the question of the scholarship was settled, he directed his attention to my travel arrangements.

Indeed, every member of the household showed such active personal interest in my imminent departure as was worthy of their noble and generous tradition. It felt as though the master of the house himself, and not a mere houseboy, was leaving. Everyone treated me as a son, and they all busied themselves over the preparations.

Aziza's interest in this matter, however, topped everyone else's. This revived my hopes a little. Often she would chatter on happily about the future, how I would come back one day, a university graduate, and find all doors open before me. She did this naturally, with her familiar spontaneous sincerity. Little did she realize how her words wrung my heart! I wanted to tell her that whatever bright prospects the future held would mean nothing without her: however much I achieved, something vital would always be missing.

There was nothing new or sudden in her attitude: Aziza has always shown interest in my affairs.

Gradually, the impatience to leave for what I regarded as my new battleground began to evaporate. As the actual time of departure drew near, a lump rose in my throat at the thought of separation from those I loved, the thought of all the dull, lifeless mornings I would have to face without the gentle comfort of Aziza's presence and her sweet voice.

I was painfully tempted during this period to own up to her and put my heart in her hands. The agony I felt at having soon to part from her gave me a kind of desperate boldness that goaded me more than once to the point of confession. But every time I opened my mouth, another voice spoke inside me, "Whatever else I may be or become, I am still an underling." It yelled, "I am an underling in the pay and debt of this family. What they appreciate in me are my purity, my impeccable behavior, and my moral scruples. Is it worth losing their good opinion in a foolish, pointless attempt at raising myself in the world?! No I must see reason! I must stick to my firm resolve to bury my feelings deep in my heart."

The family, in view of my impending departure, cut the summer holidays short, and we went back to Makkah. The night I actually said goodbye was indeed memorable: the lady of the house prayed continuously, often under her breath, and whenever she saw me fold a garment, her eyes glistened with tears. She told me over and over what a void there would be when I left, after all those years I spent with them. Sheikh Abdul-Hamid gave me a lot of instructions and repeated them several times. He instructed me on what to do, what to take along, where to live, how to budget my allowance, how to study. He also urged me not to indulge in immoral distractions, and prayed for my success and well being. Aziza wished me good luck in very moving words that did not, however, break the rules of propriety and good breeding. As for Nanny Gom'a, she raised her hands up to heaven, facing the Grand Mosque, and prayed in simple and moving words, asking God to grand me safety and success. It was impossible for me to tell them how moved I was by their feelings, and how grateful I was for them. I wanted to tell them that I was resolved not to disappoint them but to live up to their expectations.

And so, we parted.

I boarded the bus heading for Beni Faham, my village, to say goodbye to my family there. During the journey I was absorbed in my thoughts. There I was, going back to the village in a fast comfortable bus; only ten years ago my father and I had left it on foot. I had left it in happy ignorance of what awaited me in Makkah. Even the plan to hire me as a house-boy was not mentioned to me until after my first night there.

The train of memories rolled on fast: Sheikh Ba Qays, Sheikh Salah, Sheikh Abdul-Hamid, Mr. Abdul-Razik, my mistress, and Aziza. I paused long and fondly at her image as it floated up in my mind. I was now free to think of her as long and as much as I liked without fear or shame. She was far away and I could neither offend her by word nor gesture. Her beloved face, her tear-stained eyes as we said good-bye, her suppressed sobs, and heart-felt wishes accompanied me all the way. She had said, as I withdrew my hand from her grasp, "Take care, Ahmad." Then she was overcome by tears.

I went closely over the different stages of our relationship, from the moment she had said on seeing me for the first time, "Come and play," to that last, "Take care, Ahmad." I puzzled and puzzled over the nature of her feelings for me. I knew that I mattered to her a great deal, but mattered as what? I recalled my first night at night school, how she had waited up for me, how she had laughed excitedly when I had managed to read a whole sentence from what I had learnt that day. I remembered that she had sat down to correct my mistakes and held my hand to show me how to hold the pencil properly and how to draw the letters on the paper. I lingered over the memory of her enthusiastic encouragement when I got the primary school certificate, her towering joy when I obtained the secondary school certificate, and more recently, the melancholy that colored her happiness when I won the scholarship. I told myself to put aside the question of the difference in class for awhile and try to explore her real feelings away from any social considerations. The search was fruitless, for I ended exactly where I started. The exploration yielded nothing except the old firm conviction that Aziza harbored no more for me than the fraternal feelings she had once voiced. I sighed heavily, feeling more confused than ever. But my sad confusion of mind was mixed with a sense of relief: I had scrupulously guarded the honor and dignity of the family and had not injured that honor by so much as a word.

We arrived at our destination. I got off the bus and took a deep and long breath, as all the memories of childhood came rushing back.

This was the birthplace I had left as a boy of nine, naive and illiterate. I came back to it now a mature, experienced young man about to go abroad to study. So many things had happened to me in those years, things I had never foreseen. God had destined me for them, though, and it was His Mercy that led me so far.

When I pushed open the old creaking front door of our house, another emotional scene greeted me, just as the one I had left behind in Makkah. There were tears and smiles, embraces, and prayers of thankfulness. My mother put her arms round me and she rested her head on my shoulder and cried long and silently. She did not say one word, only cried. It was our first meeting in ten years. My father, after embracing and kissing me, shook hands in a manly fashion. My brothers and sisters, who were very tiny when I left, now leapt around me and hung on my clothes. I hugged them and our tears mingled with our laughter. I reveled in the gift of love God had blessed me with--the gift of loving and being loved by my real and adopted families.

We stayed up the whole night chattering and exchanging news. I related my adventures since I left the village, and spoke of my good fortune in having settled with Sheikh Abdul-Hamid. I described my arduous progress from night classes to the present juncture in my life. They listened avidly as if I was relating the adventures of the folk hero "Clever Hassan" or "Sinbad the Sailor"! When I reached the end of my narrative, my mother bent her head thoughtfully then said in a tremulous voice, "And now you'll be going again. You're leaving us again."

"Mother, please!" I pleaded, "I can't take any more! It was such a wrench having to leave Makkah. It was so painful I nearly changed my mind about going altogether. If you don't help me over this, I swear I shall give up the scholarship."

She, the simple illiterate peasant woman, understood, and at once beamed at me from a tear-stained face and said, "Of course you're going Son --God protect you. We're proud of you. It's only my pride in you that has made me cry." Father suddenly asked as if to change the subject, "By the way, what branch of study did you choose?"

"Medicine," I replied. At this, my mother exclaimed in sheer joy, "God indeed is the All-Powerful! Imagine! My son a doctor! Who could have believed it! God grant you success, my son; may His Hand always lead and guide you."

The following morning I boarded the bus going to Jeddah.

Being so near Makkah I could not resist visiting the Grand Mosque or calling once more on my foster family. I went to the Mosque first, then headed for the house and knocked at the door. Nanny Gom'a opened it and froze in utter amazement. She stared at me incredulously for a moment then began shouting in mingled joy and amazement, "Master, Master, Mr. Ahmad has come, he's come back sir!"

"Mr. Ahmad!" The words sounded strange to my ears. I had always been the "boy" or the "young man"--the servant who addressed others as masters! At her call, an instant turmoil ensued. Sheikh Abdul-Hamid ran to the door, his wife and daughter following closely at his heels. In answer to their surprised inquiries, I said jokingly, "Well, I went, got my degree, and here I am!"

Sheikh Abdul-Hamid burst out laughing and said, "God willing Son, God willing." I explained that being so near Makkah, I could not miss the chance of visiting. My eyes rested on Aziza who immediately blushed deeply and lowered her eyes. I spent the night there and left the following morning.

I set out firmly determined to make a success of my mission and realize the hopes pinned on me by everybody, especially those who helped me to take this road; in short, success had come to be an obsession. From that moment on, it became my destiny to feel at home only when I was fighting some battle.

Chapter Eleven

Chapter Eleven

It did not take long to settle down and feel at home in my new surroundings. I found lodging in a building inhabited mostly by fellow Saudi students. We lived in the Saudi manner, doing Saudi cooking, and entertaining ourselves in the Saudi style. This made the place feel very much like home. I was determined to devote

all my time to my studies, to forsake all my leaves and go home only when I qualified. I was fully aware that a medical degree was no easy matter. Besides, I was after no mean success. I wanted to distinguish myself and knew this could be achieved only through complete dedication.

Letters from home--both the village and Makkah--arrived regularly. In her letters, Aziza was careful to describe minutely all the occurrances at home, even the most trivial and insignificant details. I used to read and reread her letters, over and over, searching for something--a delicate hint of intimacy, or even a vague sign of hope. But it was a fruitless quest. Her letters were written in the same formal, straightforward manner she had always adopted when addressing me. I couldn't decide whether she adopted that detached impersonal tone on purpose, or whether it was dictated unconsciously by her natural innocence.

Time passed bringing me success upon success. I was advancing firmly towards my final goal. It's in the nature of things for correspondence to slacken after a while. The letters gradually grew shorter and far between, until they finally stopped. I was too busy to write the expected long and detailed letters in response.

For a long time there was silence. I used to reassure myself that no news was good news, that surely they would cable me if anything went wrong. I resisted the idea of going home for the summer vacation--sweet as it was I simply needed every minute of my time and could not indulge my natural cravings.

Thus, seven whole years passed without a single visit home. Then, news of Sheikh Abdul-Hamid's death reached me. The news hit me like a thunderbolt. A single idea possessed me--to leave for Makkah at once. My friends tried to dissuade me; I had only one year to go before I qualified, they said. Besides, what good would my going to Makkah do now? The man, God rest his soul, was dead after all, they argued, and I could do nothing for him now. What would be the good of going, especially as I stood to lose so much? By going I would only awaken the sorrow of the family and delay the progress of my studies.

They said that I had reached the critical pre-finals stage and any solace I could get from a quick visit to Makkah could not justify the serious damage my studies would sustain as a result. These arguments won me over and I decided against going. My conscience however would not leave me in peace. It reproached me for having neglected my family for so long, for having been lulled by the facile assurance that no news was good news. The death of Sheikh Abdul-Hamid had belied that maxim in a most dramatic and painful way. Had I stopped caring? Had I forgotten them? Sheikh Abdul-Hamid, his wife, his daughter, and Nanny Gom'a?! Had I blotted out the memory of all those happy days spent in that affectionate home? Was I selfish and self-seeking when I poured my heart and soul into my studies to the exclusion of all else? Was this the way to treat those who had been kind to me and treated me as a son? No, I thought; they had not deserved such indifference, ingratitude, and neglect. My conscience refused to be appeased by the sound common sense of my friends. Common sense did not, as usual, take into account such irrational things as feelings.

I made my way to the Scholarships Department and acquainted the director of my intention to leave for home. The man was plainly astonished, especially as I had not expressed such a desire at any time before. He said, in a voice that still held a note of incredulity, "Every student is allowed to go home on a visit every now and then. You have not as far taken advantage of these facilities and are perfectly entitled to do so now. I personally have no objection, particularly as you have proved yourself quite an exemplary scholar and young man."

I thanked him for his good opinion and hinted at my reasons for leaving, whereupon the man immediately took the necessary steps; I began to buy presents and prepare for my departure.

As the boat bore me towards Jeddah, my mind, impatient to regain home, raced forward to my destination. In Jeddah, I stopped only for half an hour, long enough to find a car to take me to Makkah. In the car I was afire with longing. I saw in my mind's eye good Sheikh Abdul-Hamid and fervently prayed for his soul, and asked God to shower His Mercy on him and make Paradise his eternal abode, for he was a generous and benevolent man, always ready to help with his money and his sympathy.

Alas! I thought sorrowfully, what bliss it would have been to be going now to meet him, to kiss his good hands, to offer him my gratitude and thanks. Ah! To have been able to show him how the little seed his good hands had planted had grown, blossomed, and was about to bear fruit!

But alas, Sheikh Abdul-Hamid was no more. He was now in the glorious presence of his Creator, having shuffled off this mortal coil and departed to the house of eternity. I prayed fervently, with all my heart, "My God, have mercy on his soul and reward him well and grant him undisturbed rest." In my prayers, I also included my own poor father.

I derived little comfort from my prayers, for they reawakened and intensified my sense of guilt. And as the car wound its way through the narrow streets and alleys of Makkah towards the Sheikh's house, my conscience was reproaching me bitterly once more.

Chapter Twelve

Chapter Twelve

I reached my destination at last. The house was unexpectedly quiet, as if deserted, and all the doors were shut. I was puzzled. The main door was always kept open during the day on account of the endless stream of callers. There was no answer. I repeated the knock more forcefully and was answered by the same heavy

silence. I grew anxious and started banging hard with both my fits until I was exhausted. But all remained still and quiet.

I stood there at a loss helplessly wondering. What could have happened? Where was everybody? My mistress? Aziza? Nanny Gom'a? Where could they have all gone? What should I do now? Where could I look for them? The idea of finding nobody at home had not crossed my mind and now took me completely by surprise. I did not know what to do or where to go. "How incredible to find the house so totally deserted!" I thought as I resumed banging the door more persistently. The answer I finally received did not come from inside. In the house opposite, a window was suddenly thrown open and a man looked out.

"Save yourself the trouble, man," he bawled at me, "There's nobody in there." I recognized the voice at once: it was Uncle Tahseen, Sheikh Abdul-Hamid's neighbor and friend. I felt like a drowning man who had suddenly found a raft.

"It's Uncle Tahseen, isn't it? Would you come down please Uncle? I'd like to speak to you. Don't you remember me? I am Ahmad, Ahmad bin Ayda." The man peered at me short-sightedly, then exclaimed, "Ahmad! How are you my son? Welcome home! Forgive me, I didn't recognize you at first. I'll be with you in a minute."

His head disappeared from the window on the second floor of his house and I waited with a thumping heart, guessing apprehensively at what he had to tell me. A few moments later, the door opened revealing Uncle Tahseen spreading his arms wide open to embrace me. As he hugged and kissed me he kept exclaiming, "How marvelous, how wonderful! God be praised! You've become a man, Ahmad. Come in, come in!"

As I accompanied him into the house, a thousand and more questions raced to my lips. We sat down and he said, "Welcome home, God be praised for your safe return. When did you arrive?"

"Only this morning, Uncle. I took the boat and we docked in Jeddah this morning. I did not stop anywhere on the way--I came straight here."

"Welcome, welcome! It's been such a long time!"

"I came as soon as I heard that Sheikh Abdul-Hamid has died. I couldn't stay in Egypt a moment longer! I thought the family might need me."

"The family?" inquired the man bitterly, shaking his head in sorrow.

Fear gripped my heart as I hastened to ask, "Do tell me please, what happened? Where is everybody? Where is the lady of the family?"

"The lady? Well, may God give you a long life."

"Dead! When? How?"

"About a year and a half ago, no, nearly two years now."

"Two years! --And Sheikh Abdul Hamid was still alive then?"

"Yes."

"And he never told me! Why? Why? She was like a mother to me, God rest her soul!"

"He insisted on keeping the news from you, God rest his soul. He wouldn't allow anyone to tell you. He knew how much you loved her. He was afraid the news would affect your studies. He kept it a secret from you until he himself joined her."

I did not dare ask about Aziza: I could not bear to hear that something had happened to her too, or that she had gotten married. Uncle Tahseen, however, saved me the trouble. He went on to answer the question that was clamoring in my mind and fighting its way persistently to my lips.

"There is only Aziza now," he said. A terrible burden fell off my shoulders. "Thank God," I whispered, as I pricked my ears.

"She has been very ill and weak since her father died. The doctors don't know what's wrong with her. Quite as a loss! Some say it's the shock of her father's death, others that she must have been ill for a long time without the symptoms showing until the disease reached a critical stage and completely overpowered her."

I was dazed by the news. "But where is she now?" I asked anxiously.

"At the Zaher Hospital. I am sure she'll be very glad to see you." I was shocked. What tricks life played on us, I thought. Like a fool I had come expecting everything to be the same save for Sheikh Abdul-Hamid's departure, only to find that the lady was dead and Aziza mysteriously sick. In agony I whispered, "God alone is All-Powerful."

The sense of helplessness that had always plagued me in my relationship with this family once more came surging back. I found myself again in the same impotent, subordinate, subservient position, unable to render help of any kind. I was cheated out of the chance to pay my debt of gratitude to the family that had supported, assisted, and loved me so well. I thought I would be able to stand by them in their hour of need with the death of the Sheikh and thereby pay back some of my debts. That was denied to me. There was no one left to help or stand by. Even Aziza was in the last stages of her illness and I could do nothing for her. It seemed as though I was doomed always to take, never to give, always to be at the receiving end.

I was completely absorbed in my sad thoughts for a while and sat there dumbly staring in front of me until I felt Uncle Tahseen's hand pulling gently at mine as he got up.

"Let's go inside my son," he said. "We'll rest for a while and have some tea, then we'll go together to visit Aziza." I raised my head sharply as if some idea had suddenly struck me, "Nanny Gom'a! Where is she, Uncle?"

"With Aziza at the hospital. She never leaves her side," he replied. I sighed in relief. Nanny Gom'a was all right then. Aziza still had her. She was not completely shorn of love and care in her sick loneliness.

We went inside. The place was familiar to me.

As a child I had often gone there and wandered all over it until I came to know it like the back of my hand. I fondly recognized the Arabian style hall, the stairs that led to the upper floors, the sweet aroma of gum and musk that perfumed the air inside. I knew how fond Uncle Tahseen had always been of that particular fragrance. The little bookcase still stood in its usual corner, and his hookah rested in its usual stand beside his favorite chair.

He led me to his private sitting room and left me, saying, "I'll leave you for a minute. I must tell Umm Umar that you're here." Umm Umar was his wife, a hospitable, kindly woman. I remembered her as she came to visit us in the old days, as she did frequently, wrapped up in her white shawl, dangling her long rosary, and forever beaming contentedly on everybody. Her face expressed contentment and inward serenity. She was always singing the name of God and His Prophet and ordered everybody to do the same. I could recall many instances of her kindness and affection and, therefore, was not surprised to hear her hurried footsteps down the stairs. Her appearance showed little change. Her grave beauty was the same. I hastened to kiss her hand. She sat close to me while Uncle Tahseen resumed his seat.

She recalled the old days with a great deal of sorrow and related all that had happened since my going away. She gave me all the facts of the lady's death in painful detail. She also described how her illness had deprived her of speech and movement due to partial paralysis, how she had fought her illness with courage and cheerful endurance, and how she had finally succumbed to it. She told me of the family's agony when they realized that her case was a hopeless one and that death might be the sole hope of relief.

In the course of her narrative she dwelt on Aziza and her news quiet noticeably. She repeated several times the fact that Aziza had turned down many suitors. I did not realize then the significance of her remarks; I was not even aware she was trying to hint at something. I simply took her words to mean that she disapproved of Aziza's behavior.

Eventually, she stopped and made no more enquiries. The room was engulfed in silence. I crept back into myself and in pain dwelt on the memories of the house that had witnessed the happiest years of my life. That house had set me a standard, so that all my efforts, all my achievements, were an attempt to rise up to it. Now it was empty, deserted of all its inhabitants, or nearly all. They had departed--some to the grave, some to the hospital. I realized then how wrong I was to stay away all those summer vacations, how selfish I was to immerse myself so feverishly in my studies. Such dedication had been rewarded by distinguished success, but my success suddenly seemed pointless. It had been purchased at the expense of duty, my duty towards my foster family.

A sigh of pain escaped me. I repeated incredulously, "How strange are the ways of God! God alone is All-Powerful!"

"Maybe you'd like to go to the hospital now," said Uncle Tahseen as he rose to his feet.

"Indeed, I would."

"Give me a moment then to get ready. I won't be long," he said as he left the room. When he disappeared behind the door, I slipped back into my former gloomy abstraction. Upon this, the lady started exclaiming, clapping her palms in a gesture of sorrow, "Poor, poor Aziza! Who could have believed it! She was like a rose spreading her fragrance all over the district!"

"There she goes again," I thought, "back on the Aziza theme." What was she trying to say? Did her words carry a hidden message? Or were they simply effusions of feeling? I was not to know the right answer until much later.

Uncle Tahseen came back in his out-of-door clothes, "Come on my son, we'll go visit Aziza and Nanny Gom'a." We made our way with heavy steps to the hospital; it felt as if I carried on my shoulders all the burdens of humanity. I shied away from the prospect of seeing that "fragrant rose" as Umm Umar had called her, bedridden and in pain.

What had I done? How could I have neglected Aziza all those years in pursuit of self-advancement? It was she, paradoxically, and my desire to make myself worthy of her, that had caused that neglect, that single-minded absorption in work. Now that I was about to lose her, what use was a degree to me? How could I have withstood being away from her those years if I really loved her?!

"But I do love her," I answered my own accusing thoughts warmly. "God is my witness, I do love her and have never loved any other. I had wanted to rise up to her level so that, one day, I might . . ." At this point my mind stopped abruptly and would not dare to go any further. I would not admit even to myself that I wanted her for my wife.

A touch from Uncle Tahseen's hand extracted me from my feverish thoughts. We had reached the hospital.

Chapter Thirteen

Chapter Thirteen

The hospital was like a bee-hive, seething with activity. There were people going in, carrying in patients who couldn't walk, and people coming out, accompanying patients who had been cured. Those wore expressions that shone with health and happiness.

My eyes wandered over the hall where we stood, looking for

the way to Aziza's ward.

"Come this way," said Uncle Tahseen. "I know the way to her room."

I followed him down several corridors until he stopped in front of a closed door. I suddenly felt dizzy, as if I was teetering on the edge of a precipice. In sheer despair, I longed to run away. I could not bear to think that I was about to see the only girl I ever loved bedridden, in the grip of an uncertain fate. Uncle Tahseen looked closely into my face and, reading my thoughts, forced a smile and urged in a low urgent voice, "This will not do Ahmad. Aziza mustn't see you like this!"

I pulled myself together, but, not trusting myself to speak, I only nodded. He pushed open the door and we went in.

Aziza lay on the bed, pale and thin. Her long soft tresses that had often enchanted me were spread across the pillow. Her eyes, though a bit sunken, were untouched by the ravages of illness and still had their former beauty; but nothing else was the same. I stared at her incredulously, in spite of myself. Was this my old Aziza? Could that thin, pale body be hers? Where had the ruddy, radiant face gone? And where had gone the healthy glow of her cheeks?!

Nanny Gom'a was dozing by the side of the bed. From her fingers dangled the eternal rosary that was a permanent feature of her. I could see that she kept a constant vigil that ignored the natural boundaries of day and night and admitted only short naps. Neither of them was aware of us as we stepped inside.

Aziza had her eyes shut and Nanny Gom'a's eyes alternately drooped and started to open in a brave struggle against drowsiness. Suddenly, her eyes stared wide open and she sprang to her feet. She had noticed us at last. She shouted in utter amazement, "Who?! Master Ahmad?! Thank goodness, thank goodness!"

She rushed to me and held my hands stifling her sobs. I could not find anything to say. I advanced to the bed, and resting my arm on the head-board, looked down, and long, into Aziza's face. Nanny Gom'a kept repeating in a voice that tinkled with joy, "God be praised for your safe return Master Ahmad, God be praised!" The commotion made Aziza stir at last. Her eyes opened slowly. At first her glance bore a vacant, uncomprehending expression. But slowly, recognition dawned in her eyes and they brightened up. She forced a wan smile to her lips and stretched towards me a shaky hand.

"Ahmad!" she said weakly. "God be praised for your safe return!" I embraced her hand in mine, pressing it affectionately, and sat together with Uncle Tahseen by the bed. I fought to find words to express my feelings or, at least, return her greeting. I only gazed at her, my eyes eloquent with all I failed to say.

No one spoke. Aziza did nothing but try to stop the flood of tears that welled up in her eyes and streamed down her face to sink into the pillow. I tried once more to speak. I wanted to beg her to spare those precious tears: they seemed to fall in my heart like burning embers. I wanted to comfort her, to console her, to tell her how much I longed for her to get well. But I was miserable, afraid, confused, and could not manage a single word. But, strangely, enough, in spite of this riot of emotions, I was happy! Aziza was here at last, beside me, with only the length of an arm, or maybe less, separating us.

After a while I was able to speak. Still holding her emaciated hand in mine, I whispered, "I pray to God you'll soon be well. I came as soon as I heard. I want to stand by you. I would do anything to help you."

Nanny Gom'a answered in a voice muffled with tears, "God bless you and reward you Master Ahmad. This is what we expected of you. You came at the right time, too."

Uncle Tahseen cleared his throat in embarrassment to draw our attention to his presence. He said with forced cheerfulness, "I seem to be quite redundant here. So, if you'll excuse me? I am sure there are many matters you'd like to discuss in private. I leave you in peace."

He left the room immediately without even waiting for an answer. We were alone, the three of us. Nanny Gom'a had managed to control herself at last; she stopped crying, and only murmured intermittently, "Thank God, God be praised."

I had kept Aziza's hand in mine all the time. Her face had acquired a strange glow. Nanny Gom'a noticed it and commented on it, her voice bright with hope, "See Master Ahmad? I haven't seen her looking so well for a long time. She had been fading, the poor thing, the apple of my eyes, withering like a rose that had been denied water."

Aziza threw her a reproachful look, then pressed my hand affectionately as if trying to tell me something. Was it that she loved me as much as I loved her? Or had she missed me as much as I missed her? A dazzling light of hope suddenly flooded my heart. It must be so, otherwise why did her face wear that glow when I came? Why did she keep her hand in mine for so long? Why did she press my hand so often? God in heaven, could it be true? Could the master and the servant join their hands in love without embarrassment?

At once, I was brought up short against all the old barriers. I remembered all my former decisions, how I was determined to suppress my feelings, to smother my passion, to observe the class barriers which I firmly believed could not be surmounted no matter how many degrees I obtained. My gratitude to her family, to whom, after God, I owed everything, had brought me back to serve and help. That, however, I told myself, did not give me the right to behave as a benefactor and take advantage of the situation. I must not get carried away, as I did on first stepping into the room, and indulge in fanciful dreams of matrimony. Whatever I had to offer had to be given in the spirit of gratitude, out of an unselfish desire to serve without expecting payment.

Silence enveloped the room, except for Nanny Goma's intermittent murmurs and the sound of the prayer beads as they clicked through her fingers.

My eyes rested on Aziza as she lay there, looking peaceful and comforted--a look that was not there when I came into the room.

I felt that to think of marrying her now, even if she was of the same mind, would be a kind of exploitation I should definitely spurn. Any proposal should have been made much earlier when she still enjoyed the luxury of her parents' care. I should have asked for her hand when her father was alive; if he had accepted, then it would have been his free choice; if, on the other hand, he had declined, then it would have been within his rights. In either case, it would have been a free decision. To propose to her now when she was ill and lonely would be an unmitigated exploitation of her weakness and a cheap one at that. If she accepted, I knew I would always be plagued by the suspicion that she was forced to it by her helplessness. If she turned me down it would be a slap on the face, which my feelings would not be able to sustain. It would deprive me of the sacred flame that had fed my determination and which was responsible for my speedy and surprising progress.

My eyes wandered back to her. She seemed to have sunk into a deep, peaceful sleep. I shifted my eyes in the direction of Nanny Gom'a. Her face was serene and contented. My coming had meant something to these two poor helpless women. That explained, perhaps, the sense of relief I was experiencing. That was worth something--my studies, even my whole future career.

I smiled at Nanny Gom'a as I gently disengaged

my hand from Aziza's. "I'll go now, Nanny," I whispered. "I'll come back tomorrow, God willing. I hope all be well."

"God bless you, my boy," she repeated, "You came at the right time."

I went in a search of the doctor in charge of Aziza. He received me in his office and welcomed me with courtesy. "If you'll pardon the question," he asked, "what's your relation to the patient? You see, I just want to know how much I should tell you."

I was at a loss as to how I should answer. If I told him that I was merely a former houseboy in her father's household, he would not trust me enough to confide in me. "I . . . I am her fiancé," I found myself unconsciously replying. With a sharpness that startled me and which he tried somewhat to control and soften, the doctor exclaimed, "Her fiancé?! Where have you been all this time man?! I have often asked whether there was a man closely related to her I could talk to! There are things I want to know. Since you are her fiancé, maybe you can give me some answers."

"I really am sorry, Doctor," I said. "Certain things kept me away . . . Well, it's a long story and I won't bother you with it now. I'll only tell you that it was only today that I knew she was ill."

"Only today!" He exclaimed, obviously astonished.

"Yes. I was abroad. I am studying medicine in Cairo. I have only a year to go before qualifying. The family kept the news from me. It was only by pure chance that I came to know it."

"I see."

"And now Doctor, could you give me an idea as to what is wrong with her?"

"Nothing," he said quietly.

"What do you mean?" I asked, quite bewildered. "She seems so ill, so worn out, so weak. Her condition is even worse than I expected."

"Listen Mr. Ahmad, you'll soon be a doctor, and you'll understand what I wanted to say. There is nothing wrong with this patient . . . I mean, physically wrong. All the medical examinations and analyses we made prove that. Still, she's really sick!"

"Pardon me. I think I know what you mean, but could you be a little bit clearer?"

"As you well know, a doctor can do nothing for his patients unless they cooperate. This is especially true of cases where psychological forces come into play."

"And you believe this is true of Aziza's case?"

"Indeed, I do. She's not helping at all. She is frightfully indifferent, doesn't seem to care what happens to her. I have urged her over and over to tell me why. She never has."

I too began to wonder why! Why should Aziza, so young, at the dawn of her life, feel that way? The memory of the way she received me only a few moments ago, of how she pressed my hand with all the force she could muster in her frail condition--a thing that she had never done before--that memory sneaked into my mind. Could it be that she . . . I didn't dare pursue the thought. I wasn't brave enough to simply ask whether she loved me, and if so, when did it start? Was it an old passion like mine? But, perhaps, I went on puzzling, perhaps her pleasure on seeing me was only due to the fact that I was the only one left of the inhabitants of the old house, with the exception of Nanny Gom'a, of course. Perhaps she only needed care and protection; maybe that is why she waved aside her former reserve and gave free expression to her feelings.

"You never said anything, Mr. Ahmad," said the doctor, startling me out of my abstraction.

"In fact . . . well . . . I never expected it was like that Doctor. Maybe if I have a little time to think I'll be able to help you," I replied, not knowing what else to say.

"I do hope so. Otherwise, we might lose the girl."

Chapter
Fourteen

Chapter Fourteen

Back at Uncle Tahseen's house I had a long session with him. His wife too was present. Uncle Tahseen had insisted that I should stay at his place while in Makkah. He would not hear of my staying at a hotel while he was around, he had said.

I too craved his company. He was the only man who could

tell me something of what had taken place in my absence. He did not, however, have much to add to what he had told me previously. Umm Umar, however, managed to intrigue me by introducing a special inflection of voice whenever Aziza was mentioned, as if she meant more than was actually said. What was she trying so hard to convey? I intended to find that out through insistent, unhurried though indirect inquiry in the course of our conversation.

My daily routine in those days was as follows: the morning was taken up by Aziza and the hospital; the evening by endless talks about her and her departed parents with Uncle Tahseen and his wife. I saw Aziza's doctors frequently to discuss the case and follow the progress of treatment. Once the doctor said to me, "It seems we are caught up in a vicious circle, Brother Ahmad. She's not making any progress. I had hoped your presence would produce a favorable change, would make her care more, try to respond, to help! I hope you won't mind my asking a personal question--is there anything wrong between you?"

"What do you mean, Doctor?" I asked, quite taken aback. "What do you expect to find out?"

"I am sorry. I didn't mean to offend you, nor do I wish to poke my nose into your private affairs. But I have to ask-- Is there some disagreement?"

"Not at all, I assure you," I hastened to reply.

He hit the desk with his fist hard in a gesture of frustration and cried, "There is something missing, a kind of missing link! What is it? I wish I knew!"

His words landed me in a maze of misty,

confused thoughts. I tried to clear them up, put them in order, arrange the events according to facts and significance. I started with Aziza's behavior during our first meeting. It clearly indicated that there was some kind of feeling. What kind, I thought? Was that feeling the missing link the doctor spoke of? But maybe the missing link was simply Aziza's need for the protection of a man, any man, in her lonely state, and she simply projected that need on me! But in what capacity could I go on looking after her, protecting her? I was within sight of my medical degree, and the improved prospect and status it carried with it. Would that capacity be as her husband? Would she marry me? Would she marry her father's servant? Could the hand of the master willingly join the hand of the servant in a life partnership?

I refused, however, to delude myself. If this understanding of the situation were correct, Aziza would have gotten better. But the doctor had said otherwise--she was making no progress. I found myself forced to conclude that my analysis was wrong at its very basis and must be put aside. I had to look for that missing link somewhere else.

A new idea hit me. Since people had little choice in matters of passion, was it possible that she loved me but was ashamed of it and therefore determined at all costs to suppress her feelings? The thought chilled the blood in my veins. I froze as the thought took root in my mind. It meant losing Aziza forever. That was the unalterable conclusion. I could never hope to marry her, and even if, by some fluke, I did, we could never be happy so long as she continued to entertain the thought of my being inferior to her.

The room swam before my eyes. I felt suddenly worn out, unable to go on thinking of this matter, inspecting its various possible angles. I felt that if I went on pursuing that maze of speculation, I would either go mad, or have a nervous breakdown!

I regained control over myself and said that it was too early to consider such complicated questions. The immediate, important job was to get Aziza back on her feet, regardless of anything else. That was my duty and I was not going to shrink from it. I felt a little comforted when I had done that. I also felt that I should trust God with the solution of this dilemma since He alone controls our destinies.

One night I said to Umm Umar, "Umm Umar. There is something I'd like you to do for me."

"Anything, my son," she answered eagerly. "What is it?"

"I want you to come along with me now. Uncle Tahseen too . . ."

"Where should we go now, my son? It's past midnight!" she asked in surprise.

"To the Grand Mosque."

"Certainly Son, but why?"

"I want to seek God and take refuge in Him at this third part of the night. I want to seek His Solace and Succour in the night, Umm Umar. I will ask Him, and He will answer, as He always answers those who are desperate, strained, baffled, or in need. He will lift evils and ills."

"Of course, my son," interposed Uncle Tahseen. "Our trust in God is indeed great. But God, my son, can hear us wherever we may be. He is closer to us than our jugular veins. He listens to us everywhere. He says, 'Call me and I will answer thee.' We can pray to Him in any place and in all places."

"Indeed, my son, I always pray for her with all my heart," said Umm Umar as if to enforce her husband's argument.

"Thank you, Aunt. But I do wish you would humor me."

"There is no harm in that. We'll make this a real Friday night, a blessed night, by the will of God."

We went to the Grand Mosque, all three of us, and made the rounds of the House of God, drank of the Holy Well, and prayed. I wept then as I had never done before in my life.

The tears streamed down my cheeks. They were the tears of an impotent and weak slave in the presence of the All-Mighty and All-Great. We awaited the dawn prayers. When they were done we left. I felt much relieved. It was as if the copious tears I had shed washed away my sorrow. I felt that God would not let me down, that He would, in the advancement of time, make my hopes come true.

At the hospital the doctor said, "Do you really want to know what I think, Brother Ahmad?"

"Of course."

"Well, I think Aziza would be much better off

at home. We can do nothing more for her here. Who knows? Maybe the home atmosphere would do the trick. Maybe she'll respond better to treatment once she is there. Of course, I will still look after her and visit her regularly."

I consulted with Uncle Tahseen and he approved of the idea. At the last minute, it occurred to me that since summer had already begun, it might be a good idea to remove Aziza to Ta'if where the air was much gentler. That could help her both physically and mentally. We suggested this to Aziza and she agreed without a moment's hesitation. We went to Ta'if.

It was my first visit to the place since that eventful, momentous summer, so many years ago when I got my school certificate.

Chapter Fifteen

Chapter Fifteen

Once in Ta'if, I tried to recreate for Aziza the same home atmosphere we had enjoyed before I went abroad. At first her gloom and depression persisted. She continued to refuse food and would only manage a few mouthfuls when Nanny Gom'a had pressed, begged, and entreated for a long time. I took her around Ta'if and

we relived the memories of the past when her parents were alive. We went to all the beautiful spots, Lea, Mathna, and Hada, and passed good times there.

The change came gradually but unmistakably. She still spoke very little, but her appetite improved and she showed a more lively response to my jests and banter. With growing relief and happiness, Nanny Gom'a and I watched her steady progress towards health, her improving appetite, her growing cheerfulness, and rising spirits. We felt hopeful and transmitted our optimism to Uncle Tahseen and his wife who frequently called upon us there.

I kept in touch with Aziza's doctor, and gave him regular reports of her progress over the telephone. He was invariably pleased at what he heard and continued to give me advice, the purpose of which I realized as a medical student.

When we left Ta'if for Makkah, Aziza had recovered completely. The so-called missing link, however, remained missing! I treated her as before and looked after her affairs like a brother; even when we joked and bantered I was careful to stick within my well-defined limits. I gave her the presents I had bought for her, her mother, and Nanny Gom'a and she took a great deal of pleasure in them. At last, I felt, everything was all right and back to normal. Only one thing remained to be done to completely settle the affairs of my family, both in Makkah and Beni Faham. To do it I had to pay a visit to Beni Faham and meet my parents.

The night I arrived, I took my father aside and

put to him what had been occupying my mind. "As you know, my father," I began, "Aziza now has nobody left in the world except God of course and us. If you and the family would move to Makkah to live near her, perhaps I could then go back to my studies. It's only a very short time to the finals."

My father thought carefully and long. "You do realize, my son," he said, "that our way of life here is vastly different from the life in Makkah or any other city. We are used to living in nature among our fields and orchards. We would feel confined and constricted in a townhouse. Besides, we are deeply attached to the land we cultivate. Take your mother. Do you know why she's still so healthy and active, like a young woman? It's the rural life we lead. It's different from the city life. No, no my son. I much prefer that we remain here."

Unsure of how things would turn out, I could not tell my father that I hoped one day to marry Aziza and that when this happened I preferred that all of us should live together. Until that moment, I was not sure and kept wavering between extremes of hope and despair. My father attributed my absorbed silence to my being hurt at his reluctance. He patted me on the shoulder and said consolingly, "The thing to do now is to go back to your studies. When you come back, who knows? Things might be different then. Leave it till the time comes."

There was nothing else to do but comply. I said goodbye to the family and went back to Makkah. I was the prey of conflicting emotions--on the one hand I wanted desperately to remain with Aziza; on the other, I felt an overwhelming desire to finish my studies. Reason told me that it would be insane to waste the effort of those years now that I was within sight of the end!

On my way back to Makkah, I was grateful I hadn't had courage to be completely frank with my father-- What had come over me, thinking I could tell him that I hoped to marry Aziza? This, however, did not clip the wings of fancy . . . I pictured in my mind what life with Aziza as my wife would be like. I quieted the reproaches of conscience by telling myself that there could be no harm in enjoying such fancies so long as they remained firmly lodged in the secret depths of my soul. In a glowing image of enchanting beauty, I saw our futures and lives joined together in an eternal bond. I saw myself as a distinguished member of the medical profession taking my wife, my partner and faithful comrade, to visit my parents in the village to show her my birthplace and the scene of my early years. I tried to imagine her first meeting my mother and sisters. They would adore her; she, too, would love them dearly. But unfortunately, as always happened whenever I indulged in such fancies, my mind interrupted my imaginings and banished them rudely.

I began to consider the best way of conveying to Aziza the news of my intended departure. I would, as usual, I thought, address her as "Mistress Aziza," then proceed to explain the matter assuring her that this time it would not be for long. Since her recovery, I had made all the necessary arrangements save some final touches that would soon be added to ensure that her life would run smoothly in my absence. A few last points remained to be settled and I could then go.

When I reached home, I was astonished to find Nanny Gom'a waiting for me in the hall of the ground floor, a very unusual thing for her to do. Before I had time to show my surprise, she embraced me anxiously like a mother and congratulated me on my safe return.

"What is it, Nanny?" I asked jokingly. "I am sure you couldn't have missed me so much. I was away only for two days!"

She looked at me thoughtfully for a moment, then said, "Come along, Son. I want to talk to you."

"By all means, Nanny," I said, "There's nothing I like better than a heart-to-heart chat."

We settled ourselves comfortably in one of the rooms and I looked at her expectantly and waited. The way she began was a little unexpected. She talked of Sheikh Abdul-Hamid and his wife, referred to the many long memories she cherished of them, and expressed her sorrow at their departure. Then suddenly, she stared at me and asked, out of sequence, "You are a young man, Ahmad; your studies are nearly finished-- Haven't you thought of marriage?"

The way the question was popped at me took me completely by surprise. I felt cornered, like a hunted quarry that had no hope of escape. I gulped several times then said in embarrassment, "To be honest

Nanny, the idea did cross my mind. But there are things, you know, things one has to do first."

"What things?" she asked with calm persistence.

I shifted my eyes away and replied with deepening embarrassment, "My studies for one thing. There's one more year to go . . ."

"That, yes. What else?" she still persisted.

I was afraid a word might escape me and reveal my secret to her. So I tried to be careful, "There is also, of course, the question of whom to marry. May God send me the woman that will make me happy."

"Are you referring to one woman in particular? Or any woman with certain qualities?"

It was not a real question. The way she put it was meant to corner me even further, and bar any attempts at evasion. I knew it was intentional and that any answer I made was bound to expose me. So I said nothing. But she, like a hunting dog, hot on the scent, said, "I am waiting . . . You didn't answer. I am sure she's lucky, whoever she may be. Have you already chosen her?"

I still said nothing. She bent towards me and gazed hard into my face, "We agreed on complete frankness, didn't we?" she asked.

"Yes . . . but . . ."

"Why don't you give me a straight answer then?"

Unconsciously, I took off the mask and pulled the screen to reveal my long buried secret.

I said impulsively and quickly, "The woman I

want is beyond my reach. I never once dared tell anybody what I felt for her."

"Who is she my son?"

"You know her."

"Aziza?" she asked calmly as if my feelings did not surprise her at all.

"Ssh . . . Not so loud."

"Why not?"

"She may hear."

"What if she did? What would happen?"

I did not know what to say. We were silent for a few moments. Then, in a voice redolent of the gentleness and warmth of a mother, she said, "Why shouldn't she hear? She's proud of you. You have been good to her. You stood by her in her hour of need . . ." This was the crux of the matter, the tangle that would not be unraveled, I thought.

"No Nanny," I said. "Please, don't get things mixed up. I did not stand by her expecting to get a reward. It was my duty. I did it out of gratitude." I paused for breath, then added, "I spent many years in the house. I received the care that only good and generous people can give. And they were--good and generous. You yourself witnessed many of the favors Sheikh Abdul-Hamid showered on me, God bless his soul. It was he who gave my life a new direction and sent me to the university. All that time I thought of Aziza as my mistress. I tried to shut out my mind any thoughts of even the possibility of making her mine. I knew there was no way."

"But why, Son? You are young and bright

with excellent prospects."

"That may be. But never forget, Nanny, that I have always lived here as an inferior, on the receiving end of the line."

My words made her sit up. She threw me a reproachful look and said in shocked, disapproving tones, "What! Inferior! Good God! I never expected to hear such rubbish from an educated man like yourself. You, my son, have never been an inferior in this house. Only those who are idle and sponge on people and live off the labors of others are inferior. Inferior people, my son, are beggars, and you have never begged of anyone but God. I have known you all your life. You have always been a proud soul and earned your living; you sweated, and those who live by the sweat of their brow are no inferiors.

"Believe me, my son, you are wrong to think this way, absolutely wrong. You shouldn't have kept your feelings a secret all these years. You should have told her. You are a man any woman would wish for, would love. You possess all the qualities people admire in a young man--education, knowledge, youth, and sound moral principles. You should thank God for all these gifts; you should carry your head high and regard life in a more practical, realistic light. I don't want to hear of this inferior business any more. You should banish it completely out of your mind. Indeed, I would go even further than that and say that if there's anything at all wrong with you, it is this feeling of inferiority.

"To discover such weaknesses in you has

shocked and distressed me. I am only an illiterate woman, or nearly illiterate. The only things I know are what Sheikh Abdul-Hamid and his wife taught me and that does not amount to much--a few verses of the Qur'an and a few prayers. Still, to see an educated man like you describe me . . . no, no, my son . . . you should discard this idea at once. You must be strong and practical besides being modest. You are at the door of a bright career. You shouldn't let such doubts and fears sneak into your mind."

I listened to this illiterate or semi-illiterate woman, spellbound. In spite of all my education, it had never occurred to me to consider my problem from this new angle. Gradually, with every spirited, zealous sentence, the picture rearranged itself and a new spirit infused me. If such wisdom, such a sound, mature view could come from this simple woman, how did I then, an undergraduate, manage to trap myself in my inferiority complex? How could I let it dominate and spoil my life all these years?! Her words shook me to the very depths of my soul; a few shadows of doubt, however, still lingered-- All my fears were not completely dispelled. For even if I believed that I was not inferior to Aziza, I could not be sure that she herself felt the same way.

"You speak very sensibly, Nanny Gom'a," I said in a shaky voice. "I may have been wrong to think this way. But Aziza . . . She could feel differently about it."

"If it is simply a question of what Aziza thinks," she interrupted spiritedly, anticipating my words, "You can go right ahead. Put your trust in God and propose to her. I can even tell you that she reciprocates your feelings."

"Is this true, Nanny? Is it true?"

"It is. She has never stopped thinking of you and talking about you since you left, never."

"But she's never even given so much as a hint! Why?"

"So many obvious reasons. For one, her feminine modesty and upbringing; for another, well . . . she thought that perhaps you had become attached to someone abroad-- You have been away for so long, you know!"

"Attached to someone else!" I exclaimed with deep feeling. "Her image never left my mind for a moment. Her love, and I don't mind saying it out loud, her love has always possessed all my feelings and sensations."

"That I know my son. She, however, spoke of this once and indirectly too. You know how proud women are. More than once I told her that I knew her secret. I even went so far as to suggest that she should tell you how she felt. But she refused adamantly."

"Well," she added with a sigh, "here we have two silly young people, deeply in love, but refusing to admit it to one another, preferring to suffer, each one alone."

"But I have explained to you, Nanny . . ."

"Explained? What have you explained? Have you forgotten that the Prophet himself married

Khadijah after working for her and found nothing to embarrass or shame him in that? You are educated and you know that the conduct of the Prophet should serve as an example for us!"

"Ah Nanny! I never saw things this way before! You make everything, all forbidding obstacles, so easy, so simple!"

"Never mind that. Now tell me, do you wish to marry the girl?"

"I think you already know the answer."

"Leave it to me then."

"How? What are you going to do?"

"I'll speak of the matter with Umm Umar. I'll suggest to her that Uncle Tahseen should suggest it to Aziza."

"Umm Umar! You remind me of something that has often puzzled me."

"What?"

"She spoke to me more than once in the same vein you took, telling me what a wonderful girl Aziza was, and who, she wondered, would be the lucky man to have her . . . It made me wonder sometimes."

"No wonder she did! In fact, I expect she'll have talked to Aziza by now as I have talked to you."

"I'll leave the matter in your hands then, and I'll never forget this kindness."

"It is no kindness, Son; it is my duty towards the two of you. All I ask for is that you forget all this inferiority nonsense and become strong and self-confident."

"I promise, Nanny . . . I swear," I said overpowered

with joy.

She patted me on the shoulder once more, took me by the hand and led me upstairs. Aziza was sitting in front of the window that overlooked the garden. She gave us a charming smile as we went in and welcomed us. We chatted in the usual way about the weather, how the summer was nearly gone, the climate of Makkah in the winter, and how I missed it when I was abroad . . .

Only my tongue took part in the conversation. My mind dwelt on how closer than ever Aziza was to me now: in the past she had seemed out of reach; now that I had finally overcome my feelings of being inferior to her, she seemed so near. It only remained for Uncle Tahseen to talk to her.

I was afraid that by a gesture I would betray my excited mental state. So, I made some excuse and left. That night, Nanny Gom'a made my bed in the library on the ground floor, where the former master of the house, Sheikh Abdul-Hamid, used to sleep.

Chapter
Sixteen

Chapter Sixteen

Everything went according to plan. Nanny Gom'a arranged the matter with Umm Umar who was overjoyed at the news, as I later heard. She had sighed in relief and said cheerfully, "At last he made a move, that young man. They suit each other so well, those two."

Umm Umar, in her turn,

talked to her husband and he, too, was very pleased. He paid us a call the following morning, and winking at me, he asked to see Aziza on very important business. I blushed deeply and thought it better to leave the house before the interview was over. I went out telling Uncle Tahseen that I would call on him at his place after the noon prayers. I wandered aimlessly through the streets of Makkah. I felt very tense and agitated, for at that moment, I felt, Uncle Tahseen was talking with Aziza, settling the hope of a lifetime for the both of us, the hope that had worried and eluded me for so long.

My feet led me to the café I visited with my father on our first day in Makkah. I felt a strong urge to spend some time there drinking tea in my own special way and rearranging my thoughts and my view of the future in the light of these latest developments. A deep sense of contentment and well-being swept over me: my long-borne burden had slipped off my shoulders at last.

I started going over all the events of my life, pausing long at the ones where Aziza figured. I discovered to my surprise, that looked at in this new light, they accorded with Nanny Gom'a's interpretation. Nanny Gom'a had revealed to me the missing link the doctor had talked of, and for which I had searched long and fruitlessly. It consisted simply of a pure spiritual bond between two hearts that both hadn't had the courage to confess. Aziza had harbored for me the same affection, had wished to become my wife, but her modesty and upbringing had restrained her from declaring her feelings.

 I, shackled by my sense of inferiority, had done the same.

"Was I wrong?" I asked myself. "Should I have told Aziza long ago and spared us both all this suffering?" The answer was a firm and prompt no. What I did was the only conduct that bettered a man sensible of the favors shown to him and conscious of his debt of gratitude. Besides, suppose I had told her and she hadn't responded?-- What then? It would have only detracted from my sense of duty towards her father. Yes, it had been right, and I had no regrets. It had been easier to bear the suspense of not knowing than face the possibility of her indifference.

I sighed with relief. Everything had turned out well. The missing link had been found and good news awaited me at Uncle Tahseen's house. Thank God for everything. I finished my tea, paid for it, and made my way in hurried steps towards Uncle Tahseen's house.

∗　　∗　　∗

It looked as if the man had been waiting for me at the door to give me the news, for at the first knock the door opened at once and he appeared to let me in wearing a broad smile. I read the hoped-for answer in his smile before he uttered a single word. Umm Umar was waiting for me in the sitting room. Her face too reflected joy and contentment.

"It took only a minute or two to settle the matter, God be praised." That was Uncle Tahseen's opening sentence before he launched a full account of the interview. "As soon as I told her of the purpose of my visit," he went on to say, "she closed her eyes and relaxed contentedly in her seat as if that was what she'd been waiting for for years."

"God be praised," I whispered in the depths of my heart, "God be praised."

"You are a funny pair, the two of you," Umm Umar put in. "To keep your feelings a secret for so long, to suffer so much, when you could have been the happiest couple in the world years ago!"

I did not wish to launch into another explanation of my reasons. I had turned over that page of the past once and for all with the last word of my interview with Nanny Gom'a. Besides, it was a very private matter that one did not wish to discuss everywhere. I simply said, "Well, there were circumstances Umm Umar; I was busy with my studies as you know, and . . ." '

"Studies!" she sniffed. "What's that got to do with it? Why should your studies stop you from marrying? I would have you know, my son, that Aziza, on more than one occasion, confessed her feelings to me. How she cried over my shoulder the day you left! She feared the nanny might out of loyalty, of course, tell her parents. She confided in me alone. I knew then what a noble, great passion she had for you. You don't know how pleased I was at your coming back on her father's death; and when I saw terror leap into your face at the mention of her illness, I was even more pleased. I nearly told you that day, only she had enjoined me to secrecy and made me swear to it. Not even my husband knew."

"And they say that a woman cannot keep a secret!" commended Uncle Tahseen jokingly.

We laughed and she went on, "I felt bound to protect her secret, but I also wanted to see her dream come true. I felt confident that it was destined, by the will of God, that her recovery should be at your hands, especially since she had lost her parents and had no one to turn to but God Almighty. And God has granted her wish."

During the short silence that followed, peace and contentment filled the room. It was broken by Uncle Tahseen asking, "And now, what are your plans?"

"Arrange for the wedding and the marriage contract," I answered promptly.

"Fine. God's blessing," tailed Umm Umar.

Uncle Tahseen and I echoed the prayer. The three of us felt as if the matter had been settled and what remained was merely routine--arranging for the wedding ceremony. The routine, however, kept us extremely busy for the following two weeks. I went to my village and broke the good news to the family. My father was incredulous at first. "You mean Aziza, the daughter of Sheikh Abdul-Hamid?" he asked doubtfully.

"Yes father, the very same."

"God be praised. His bounty is limitless," he said in a deeply moved voice with tears in his eyes as he lifted his face to Heaven. My mother, proud of her offspring, said, "You have turned into a man any woman would be proud to wed. In a year you will insha'Allah be a doctor." She followed her words with the traditional loud shrill of joy which announced the news to the whole village.

I brought my father and mother and eldest sister back with me to Makkah and they stayed in our house with all due honour. I was glad to see that my mother and Aziza took to each other at once. They kissed and embraced affectionately, and it was the same with my sister.

Things went as smoothly as I had hoped. The wedding was a simple affair in which the guests of honour were my father, Uncle Tahseen, and Sheikh Ba Qays.

Thus, the page of unhappiness, doubts, and pain was turned over for good. I looked forward to the future with hope and confidence now that Aziza was my wife. Yes, she was my wife!

The ceremony ended, and my people went back to the village.

Chapter
Seventeen

Chapter Seventeen

Aziza and I sat together to discuss our future plans. I told her of my intention to return to Cairo to resume my studies and complete the final stage, adding that she could join me there.

"Look Ahmad," she said smiling sweetly, "you are now my husband and your wish is my command. But, I do wish to stay

behind. There is something I should like to do while you are away." I inquired what it was and she replied, "When I was in the hospital, I often thought of the old house--this house--and the bad state it has fallen into since my father's death. I promised myself that if I recovered, and God granted my other wish, I would repair it and make it as it was before."

"And what was that other wish?" I asked. "To be yours, and make you mine," she answered, returning my smile. She paused, then, bending her head shyly, added, "God has granted our wish and we must recreate the old house in its former glory. To do this, the house has to become once more a center of learning, attracting students and other scholars from everywhere to consult and study the precious books and manuscripts its library contains--just as they did in father's time. I'd like to set one day a week for visitors to come to the library, and assign somebody the job of looking after them and giving them food and refreshments."

The picture she had drawn of the house in those few sentences was one I well remembered from the old days. The house had been a cultural center in its master's lifetime.

"You can start straightaway. Whatever you do will please me."

While we were talking, Nanny Gom'a walked in. She paused by the door and, her face working with emotions, said in a moved voice, "God be praised. This is truly a wonderful sight. God has granted that I should see you joined at last. I am sure your parents, Mistress Aziza, are sleeping contented-ly now in their graves. God has saved you from danger and favored you with a great gift."

"You regard me then as a gift, Nanny Gom'a?" I said jokingly. "This is a great kindness, but also a grievous exaggeration."

"By no means an exaggeration," she retorted warmly. "Her parents were good people, and you are their reward."

"Yes, they were good. God reward them for their goodness and their kindness to us. You were both a mother and a friend to me. It was your help and advice that brought us to this happy end. Let's say, you were a good adviser--an excellent one."

"Adviser? Me?"

We laughed. I thanked God with every fiber of my being for this flawless happiness. As we resumed discussing our plans for the house, a knock came at the door.

Our visitor was Mr. Abdul-Razik, who had fathered the idea of sending me to the university and helped a great deal to bring it to fruition. He had been away in Riyadh when the marriage took place, he said, and, therefore had not seen the invitation card we sent to his Makkan address. He came to us now, he continued, only to offer his congratulations and best wishes. We chatted on various subjects and he complimented me on the excellent reports of my progress, which he regularly received as a principal officer in the ministry of education. Then he inquired of my plans, and whether I intended to let my wife accompany me.

"Indeed that was my original plan," I replied. "I told Aziza, but there are things to arrange, matters she wants to attend to here."

He thought for a while, then said, "Listen Son. An idea has just occurred to me. It could solve this problem."

"I am all ears. I shall never forget that it was one of your sudden inspired ideas that sent me to the university."

"This is your final year, isn't it?"

"Yes."

"The final year is usually spent in practical medical training at a hospital under supervision, isn't it?"

"Exactly."

"You could do it here, in one of our hospitals. The country has developed a great deal over these last few years. We have good hospitals, and many visiting professors work here under long contracts. One of them could supervise you."

"Would that be possible?"

"It is in order, if that is what you mean. The regulations allow for such arrangements to be made. Leave it to me."

"Once more I am deeply in your debt."

"Don't say that. We are all in God's debt. Leave the matter to me. I'll get in touch with you in a few days and tell you what's been arranged."

I raced with the news to Aziza when he left. Her face glowed with happiness when she heard, and she said, "How generous You are to us, God! Now our happiness is complete. Nothing will separate us again, ever."

Shortly afterwards, I received a letter from the university notifying me that my application to spend my final practical year at a Saudi hospital had been accepted giving sundry details concerning the matter. Only one month before, I had been the prey of worry, hopelessness, and misery, at a loss what to do, possessed and controlled by false scruples. And now all my dreams, big and small, had, by the Will and Grace of God, come true. I was going to stay in Makkah and arranged my affairs accordingly. Aziza started to carry out her noble project and gathered together all her father's former students and prose-lytes. I sought them in the Grand Mosque, every single one of them, and told them of our intention to resume the old tradition. When they came to the house, it was such a moving sight that seemed to bring back the good old days.

I took charge of them myself, and arranged for their tuition at the hands of some learned men who were friends of Sheikh Abdul-Hamid. The house was once more a center of virtue and culture. We even had some young men from Indonesia who came to study the Arabic language! The house was now exactly what it had been in Sheikh Abdul-Hamid's days. It resumed, once more, its busy, cheerful atmosphere, and nothing made us happier than to see our students coming and going as before.

*   *   *

At this point, I am about to conclude this record of the memories of a lifetime--a record written intermittently, whenever my busy work as a doctor allowed me some spare time. I now have all that a man could wish for. Near me sits my son, "little Abdul-Hamid," whom God has gifted us with, playing with Nanny Gom'a, while Aziza is busy over her needlework. My eyes stray to the garden, now in full spring, colorful, and humming with birdsong. The garden has always looked and sounded just like that in spring time. Twenty years ago, the same sight and sound had greeted the senses of a little boy called Ahmad bin Ayda as he crossed the threshold of this house, to step into an undreamed of future.

I steal a look at Nanny Gom'a, as she sits there cuddling little Abdul-Hamid, and I shake my head in wonder! It was this illiterate woman who relieved a university man from the burden of inferiority, and taught him that the worth of a man is measured by his effort and his conduct; that when one is an active member of the society, a sense of inferiority is a mere delusion. A man is as big as his capacity to give earnestly of himself and his effort, to his people and to his community, and to life in general.

About the Author

Dr. Mohammed Abdo Yamani was born in Makkah in 1939 where he received his primary and secondary education. At an early age, he published short stories in local newspapers. He holds a B.S. in science from Riyadh University, Saudi Arabia, and a Ph.D. in geology from Cornell University, Ithaca, New York. Though he descended from a simple Makkan family, Dr. Yamani has managed to build a distinguished career for himself, both as a writer and as a government official. He has occupied various posts including Professor of Sciences under the Saudi Secretary of Higher Education, and Rector of King Abdul Aziz University, Jeddah, Saudi Arabia. He held the position of Saudi Minister of Information from 1975 through 1983.

Besides his short stories, Dr. Yamani has also written four novels. A Boy from Makkah is his first novel to be published in English.